To
Africa
with
Love

Also by Carroll Baker

Baby Doll
A Roman Tale

To Africa

a true romantic adventure by

CARROLL

with Love

BAKER

DONALD I. FINE, INC.   New York

Library of Congress Catalogue Card Number: 85-81868
ISBN: 0-917657-54-3
Manufactured in the United States of America
10 9 8 7 6 5 4 3 2 1

This book is printed on acid free paper. The paper in this book
meets the guidelines for permanence and durability of the Committee on
Production Guidelines for Book Longevity of the Council on Library Resources.

Map of East Africa courtesy of the
East African Wildlife Society.

Acknowledgments

I wish to thank Enrico Mandel-Mantello for allowing me to use his exceptionally fine animal photographs. He is a friend with whom I've had the privilege of sharing much, not the least of which is our mutual affection for Africa. His photographs serve as a badly needed supplement to my own. Of the hundreds of photographs I have taken, perhaps only twenty-five are worthwhile enough to accompany the text. Mr. Mandel-Mantello is an investment banker and his hobby is photography.

The lovely pictorial map of East Africa is the property of the East African Wildlife Society, the original of which is in color. Copies of it may be obtained by writing to their headquarters where you may also obtain a membership along with their bimonthly magazine on conservation: SWARA. The society's address is:

East African Wildlife Society, Mezzanine Floor, International Hilton, Nairobi, Kenya, East Africa.

EAST AFRICA

INDIAN OCEAN

TANZANIA

TENTS
LODGES
GAME RESERVES
NATIONAL PARKS
SANCTUARIES

Foreword

I made my first trip to Africa in 1964 to film *Mr. Moses,* in which I starred with Robert Mitchum. Shortly into the filming, the world press was accusing me of having an affair with Mitchum (which caused a serious rift in my marriage to Jack Garfein). Readers of my book *Baby Doll* will remember how, in truth, I was struck by Mitchum's apparent sexual availability, by the way in which, in the seclusion of the bush country, he strutted bare-chested on the porch of his bungalow, only a whisper away from my own; how when I finally went for the first time into his bungalow it was not for lovemaking but for martinis with him and Shirley MacLaine, who had arrived on a clandestine visit. Not knowing of his special friendship with Shirley, the press had assumed that it was Mitchum and I who were lovers. Alas, I never had the pleasure. And Bob's comment on the romance rumors had been: "I'm sorry I missed that."

Nevertheless, I had, indeed, fallen in love—but with Africa. Once having stepped foot there, I developed an insatiable passion for the so-called dark continent.

In 1968 the pattern of my life changed. My marriage broke up, and with my children I moved to Rome, my career having switched away from Hollywood and onto the European filmmaking scene. In the years that followed I found myself with a new freedom and more money than I had ever had in Hollywood. From Italy the flight to Africa was a shorter one, and I never missed an opportunity to return there. Once in a while, between films, with only a few days to spare I flew to Nairobi simply because I was missing it, and one Christmas I even went as chaperone to twenty-three children in addition to my own.

Perhaps for everybody there is one experience which always looms vividly above the rest. For me it was the trip I made in 1971. It not only embodied more adventure than any other, but was memorable because of the youth with whom I went. He was an extremely unusual young man, and although sixteen years my junior, he taught me to look at life with a wider vision.

This trip is my story. Our long journey took us to Kenya, the Seychelles, Tanzania, Zambia, Rhodesia, Uganda, and into the Congo to visit the pygmies. It is the story of how the native tribes reacted with profound instinct to an epileptic—of all the zany and touching and dangerous adventures his loony behavior led us into —and the love affair that developed and flourished so long as we were away from civilization.

The trip itself had much that was special about it. For one thing it was the last I was to make before the face of the continent changed forever. The familiar-sounding names of Rhodesia, Tanganyika, and the Congo were still in use. Nineteen seventy-one was perhaps the last year in which to sample the atmosphere which the early explorers had known. For much of Africa it was the last year of innocence—before skyscrapers and hot-air balloon safaris . . . and, more significantly, before the horrors of the likes of Idi Amin.

The "love" in the title is dual: enduring affection for a continent, and for the memory of a young man. Ours was a love destined from the very beginning not to last. But there are periods in our lives that live with us forever. And this was one such time for me.

Most of the photographs accompanying the text are my own. I now wish I had been more professional in my approach to picture taking. Certainly if I'd known I would one day write this book, I would have invested in more sophisticated equipment. And not having a zoom lens meant at times getting dangerously close to my subjects. On the other hand, any apprehension on my part was always overcome by the thrill of the nearness of the animals in the wild.

Geographically the narrative is precise, but I have changed the names of people and of establishments. It is the experiences, feelings, and devotion to Africa that I wish to share.

ABOVE: My first meeting with the Masai warriors during the filming of "Mr. Moses." *Photo credit: Terence Spencer*
BELOW: A bare-chested Robert Mitchum strutted about the bungalows in the village where we stayed, but I fell in love with Africa.

ABOVE: Fellow actor Alexander Knox and I visit the Tsavo Savannah—my first trip there.
BELOW: My make-up man and hairdresser created a Masai look for me to send back to Hollywood.

CHAPTER ONE

As the year 1970 was drawing to a close, I found myself feeling dissatisfied and restless. I was at the end of a love affair and perhaps feeling a bit sorry for myself as well, because I was missing everything about my ex-lover. At the time I was living in Rome, making Italian movies, but was between engagements. I was going to be alone for the holidays because I had just put my son and daughter on an airplane. The children spent every other Christmas with their father in Los Angeles. At those times the marble hallways of my Via San Valentino apartment rang coldly hollow like some deserted museum.

Then some friends asked me to share a chalet in St. Moritz over Christmas and New Year's, and that seemed an agreeable way of warding off the holiday blues. And it was in St. Moritz, while I was attending a costume party at the Palace Hotel, that I met a remarkable young man. He was to guide me toward sensuality and adventure, to gift me with an indelible memory of a journey and a romance which gave life added richness. I shall call him Sheldon, for it has the flavor of his true name.

Not knowing of the Palace Hotel's party in advance, it had not occurred to me to pack a costume, so I had spent the day making myself into a 1960s flower child by means of twisted crepe paper and artificial flowers. At the party I got separated from my friends, and it wasn't until I was desperate for a visit to the ladies room that it suddenly dawned on me—I would have to be completely unwrapped. For that I needed assistance, but no one seemed to be speaking English (or even Italian, in which I had become passably fluent.) All I could hear was a babble of German and French. My German is nonexistent and my school French doesn't go much beyond "Où est la toilette?" Anyway, it was a delicate matter, one which I felt I could best explain in my native tongue.

My distress was becoming acute and I leaned against a pillar for support. Although the organizers had requested that everyone keep their identity secret until midnight, I felt I had to take off my mask in order to dry my forehead. A beautiful pair of legs in a grass skirt approached me. Taking in the whole person, I saw a hideous African witch-doctor head covering the face and hair. The muffled voice that emerged from the mask had a neutral timbre. "Miss Baker, are you well?"

As the person recognized me, I was bold enough to say, "You speak English . . . thank heavens . . . would you do me a favor and come to the ladies room with me?"

It wasn't until we had been in a cabinet and I had been unwrapped and wrapped again that Sheldon removed the witch-doctor head and introduced himself. His behavior during my unveiling had been completely matter-of-fact. Perhaps that was why I hadn't divined his masculinity. He had treated me as a person in need and had come to my rescue unhindered by convention.

Upon seeing him unmasked at the wash basins, the other ladies quickly left the room. Sheldon hardly noted their reaction. But I suddenly saw how funny the situation was and began laughing.

We had the rather elegant ladies room to ourselves for a time and it was good to be away from the noise of the party. I was intent upon talking to this young man. His behavior was quite out of the ordinary and the things he said fascinated me. For someone of his age, he seemed wildly eccentric.

I found myself noticing how handsome he was, but I reminded myself that I must not be too attracted to him. After all, I was a mature woman and he was obviously still a boy. My guess was that he was in his early twenties, perhaps fifteen or sixteen years my junior. But oh, he was so lovely. In appearance he reminded me of a Renaissance painting of a saint. He was slight of build but not overly thin . . . fair complexioned, yet not pale . . . gentle, without seeming weak.

I examined his witch-doctor head, which was resting on the a wash basin. It looked authentic. I told him of my keen interest in African artifacts.

"Me too," he said. "I've been to Africa many times."

"Have you?" I said. "So have I, and not only to make movies."

Slowly and carefully he raised a hand and softly stroked my cheek. He studied my features with an expression close to wonderment, as if he had discovered the world's most precious object. I remembered speaking to him inside myself: "Go ahead and flatter my pride. Make me feel in my womanly summer's end that I am irresistible to young boys."

He said, "I'm going to Africa again shortly. Will you come with me?"

It was so charming, and he had such a radiance as he asked me that question. A total childlike belief that every wish could come true. He had met a movie star transformed for the moment into a flower child, and together they would set out on a great adventure to a far distant land.

For an instant I actually wanted to abandon myself and blurt out, "Yes," but I hesitated just long enough for the practical side of my nature to take over and replied instead with a rather dubious, "Perhaps."

I couldn't refrain from spending a great deal of time with Sheldon over that Christmas holiday. I had found him surprisingly easy to be with. He was interesting and fun, and all those things that make us like another's company.

To my great delight he developed a youthful ardor for me and began speaking in words of love. I had been enjoying the courtship far too much to spoil it by saying something out of a soap opera such as: "But my dear boy, I'm approaching forty and you're what? Twenty-three?" Instead I explained to him that I had escaped to Switzerland to recover from a broken love affair in Italy. He seemed to understand. Wickedly, I relished the way he struggled to contain his passion. But I, too, remained totally fascinated by him as he was with me.

There was something else which I still recall about our first encounter. But have I made it up in retrospect? Or did I indeed sense some strange, other-worldly dimension about him . . . as though his consciousness were at times on another plane? Was this strange sense I had perhaps a racial memory—did I share an ancestral belief in the magical powers attributed to the epileptic? For I did not know until some time later that he suffered from epilepsy.

The ancients would have termed Sheldon a "loony," believing as they did that epilepsy was controlled by lunar magnetics. Affectionately, I referred to him that way myself. Perhaps Sheldon's epilepsy did contribute to his being so utterly original. But his rash impulses were not irresistible to him, as they are with truly crazy people. Sheldon's impulses were simply not resisted. By choice, he lived in a world fashioned almost entirely in his own head.

I gathered he was a constant embarrassment to his socialite Parisian mother. At home in Paris with his *maman,* he told me he could be counted on to spoil her formal dinners by appearing, perhaps, in a cherry red waistcoat and pantaloons with a white ruffled blouse—or as an Arab sheik in flowing robes—or as whatever character had entered his overactive imagination on that particular day.

He had received a small inheritance for his twenty-first birthday and promptly invested it in a rundown castle in Spain. The interior was empty save for an enormous medieval wooden bed that hung from the ceiling on chains. Sheldon's first concern had been in restoring the moat and drawbridge. I'm afraid I thought Sheldon had only made up his castle in Spain, but then to my amazement he produced a detailed book of photographs as proof.

Sheldon had been raised in France, and quite naturally French was his first language. But his father was British, so Sheldon also spoke English, moreover with a charming, cultured accent. I never had a clear picture of his father. I knew only that the family was in the banking and brokerage business, and that they refused to allow Sheldon to be involved with it. Sketchy descriptions and fleeting references slipped haphazardly into Sheldon's conversation, leaving a number of facts about his life unclear to me. But then, he took strong medication twice daily to slow down his racing brain.

His epilepsy had been discovered at age five. A nasty fall had induced his first convulsion and subsequent blackout. He had been astride the balcony railing one flight up, brandishing his toy sword at a deck full of pirates. One of those imaginary pirates had administered a blow which had sent him flying over the landing, crashing down onto the parquet floor. At least, that is the way Sheldon chose to relate the story of his first experience of *grand mal.*

Travel was his passion. He could recount with great enthusiasm visits to exotic places like Bali or Fiji, and his favorite shoulder bag had come from Katmandu. Although his family kept their only child on a rather strict allowance, they never failed to provide him with those around-the-world air tickets. I speculated that they might have been only too happy to have him occupied in his travels and safely absent from family business decisions.

I suppose I must have found his helplessness appealing, particularly in those moments when he exuded the quality of a melancholy orphan. Most often, however, I felt him to be a formidable personality and one which, without guile, imposed a demand for respect, even admiration. Certainly I appreciated the fact that despite his wild flights of fancy, he never was guilty of the boisterousness often associated with the uncertainty of youth. For Sheldon was consistently well-mannered and soft-spoken. He managed to carry off even the most extravagant behavior with remarkable dignity. If his style was exotic, it was also elegant. Unwittingly I arrived at the point of becoming rather dangerously attached to him.

And so when we parted just after the beginning of 1971, I had said good-bye with deliberate restraint. I had returned to my home in Rome, planning to make a concerted effort to put the events of the holidays aside, reasoning that I had been merely swept away by the emotions of the season. I certainly had not made plans to meet Sheldon again or resume a relationship which had been fraught with amorous temptations.

CHAPTER TWO

I t was my habit to fly off to Africa without much of an excuse, and Sheldon had little difficulty convincing me to go with him in January of 1971. I had become so very, very fond of him, and as far as time was concerned there was nothing standing in my way. My next film commitment was not until spring and the children, whose private school allowed for long holidays, were not due back from California for another two weeks. I had a staff capable of handling domestic affairs, and if the children returned before I did, they were old enough to look after themselves, needing only minimal supervision. My daughter Blanche was fifteen, and my son Herschel would be celebrating his fourteenth birthday before he left Los Angeles.

Our Roman apartment was very grand, consisting of one entire floor of a palazzo in the Parioli district. In those days there did not

seem to be any difficulty in maintaining seven rooms, three bath-
rooms, double servants' quarters, and four terraces.

One of those terraces was outside my bedroom suite. It was from
there, while I was having breakfast and taking advantage of an
unusually warm January morning that I saw a black-hatted, black-
caped figure walking up Via San Valentino. Naturally the sight
intrigued me, so coffee cup in hand, I went to the railing and leaned
over to take a better look. He stopped at the flower stall on the
corner. His back was to me and his face was hidden by the large
brimmed hat. I might have guessed it was Sheldon, but I had left
him in St. Moritz only days before, and he had mentioned nothing
about coming to Rome. In fact, he was an avid skier and the snow
was wonderful that year, so he had talked about staying in Switzerland through the end of the month.

It was not characteristic of the Italians to observe such a mus-
keteer-style ensemble without hooting, but when he turned with
his newly purchased flowers the black-costumed figure paused,
and I could see why no one felt inclined to laugh. There was
something regal in his demeanor. Perhaps it was the casual way he
flipped his cape or the ease with which he observed those observing him, but he projected an elegance which was worthy more of
admiration than derision.

His black cape billowing, it looked almost as though he were
flowing across the street in a single motion. Fascinated drivers had
stopped their cars, allowing him the right of way. Pausing midway
in the traffic, he lifted his head until his eyes met mine on my
fourth-floor balcony. Sheldon smiled at me and I wondered if I
were in some sunlit dream. I hadn't noticed him searching for a
house number or counting the terraces before mine. He removed
the wide-brimmed hat with a flourish, indicated the flowers, then
proceeded toward the entrance of the building.

I spoke to the butler on the intercom to tell him that we were
expecting a visitor and that I would open the front door myself.

Then I rushed into the hallway, not quite understanding why I felt so breathless and flustered. When the doorbell rang, I hesitated before answering in an effort to compose myself. Perhaps this would mean the beginning of a love affair and I still wasn't sure if I were ready to chance a relationship with a younger man. It also occurred to me that I would have died of embarrassment had my children been at home.

By the second ring I was obliged to open the door or my butler Dominico would have appeared, thinking he had misunderstood my instructions.

The moment I opened the door, Sheldon swung me off my feet, crushing both me and his bouquet. After kissing me on both cheeks, he put me down and placed the flowers in my arms. Then he reached into his shoulder bag and produced two envelopes, fanning them in the air for me to see.

"Here are our tickets to Africa!" he said with an excitement too big to be contained. "We leave tomorrow morning."

I may have thought fleetingly of protesting about the suddenness of the trip, but I didn't because he was vibrant, full of joy, and his mood was wholly contagious. I gazed at his handsome face, into those shining eyes, and lost sight of any objections I might have had. And I sensed that Sheldon considered the matter settled.

Swooping the large hat in front of him, he bowed. Rising again, he opened his arms and invited me to dance. We began waltzing down the long marble hallway in celebration of our journey. Each time we spun by one of the archways leading into the sitting room we were spotlit by sunbeams streaming in from its bordering terrace.

In the bright flashes of light, it suddenly struck me: I found Sheldon's eccentricity enchanting and wished to confine it to us, away from the harsh scrutiny of others. He was not only original and charming, but the sum of his qualities made him endearing. And, of course, he possessed the irresistible sweetness of youth.

With each circle of the waltz I permitted myself to relax a bit more, until I was floating as one with the movement and laughing with the sheer pleasure of the physical release.

"Let's go to your bedroom," he said.

I stopped dancing. "Why?" I asked cautiously.

He grinned and replied, "Because I am going to help you pack."

CHAPTER THREE

When we arrived at Nairobi Airport, we were stopped by Customs and Immigration and asked to step to one side. Sheldon was still wearing his musketeer outfit. I was afraid at first that because of the way he was dressed they were going to search us for drugs. We sat down on a nearby bench and waited nervously until all the other passengers had been cleared. Then an official approached and told us there was a problem with the passports: neither of us had a visa. It was a formality which both Sheldon and I had overlooked.

I turned to Sheldon, about to scold him for rushing me into this trip, when I noticed that something was wrong with him. He seemed listless and vague. I took his hand and while he looked at me and responded when I spoke to him, he seemed almost to be sleepwalking. Sheldon had talked about these losses of awareness, and at times I thought I had witnessed some brief lapses in attention. Perhaps worry or emotional upsets triggered the ailment.

Petit mal is not necessarily serious but this was the worst possible time for a seizure. I didn't want the Immigration officials to notice that Sheldon was behaving oddly, and I had to think of a way of handling the visa situation.

Several officials gathered around us. Each studied the passports and then shook their heads. It was a Saturday and the embassies were closed. I didn't know what happened in a case like ours, but I feared that they might either put us back on a plane or suggest some period of detention. Above all I was afraid that if Sheldon continued to be placed under emotional strain, his condition might worsen into an attack of *grand mal.*

I had friends in Kenya, Sally and Michael MacKenna, who ran the Tsavo Game Lodge. I believed that they might be Kenyan citizens. I requested that someone call Tsavo and ask the MacKennas to vouch for us. Some minutes later a man returned and explained that Immigration would have to retain the passports. We were, however, given temporary entry permits and instructed to go to Government House on Monday to arrange visas and have our passports returned to us.

On the two-lane highway into Nairobi there are stone walls framing either side. They are trellised in brilliantly colored bougainvillaea. For me it is a beautiful, familiar sight, and normally my excitement at being back begins at this point. But after the airport ordeal, I felt drained.

Sheldon leaned over and studied my expression for a moment and then said, "I think I must have missed something back there at the airport. Was I out of it?"

"I'm afraid so."

"Sorry."

The ride into the city is a short one, and when we arrived I was surprised as ever to see how quaint and colonial Nairobi appeared. As late as the beginning of 1971, there were only a few well-lit streets and the buildings were still mainly of one and two stories. The Hilton rose above everything else in view, and as we passed by, I secretly wished that we were stopping there. Sheldon abhorred being near the usual tourist groups, but I was feeling weary and not in much of a mood to rough it at the hostel Sheldon had chosen for us. Nevertheless I had promised him that I would at least consider the rooms he had booked.

The hostel had a rather unique atmosphere—an old-world charm, and it looked clean. But there was only one bathroom and that was in the hallway. There are times when I am loathe to give up my comforts and that was one of them. I telephoned the Hilton, where they made a room available for me, and then Sheldon accompanied me while I checked in.

He didn't seem to resent my decision. I could tell that he was disappointed, but he made every effort to be accommodating and polite. He took the rejection so gracefully that I felt guilty for being so spoiled. At first I was concerned about his going back to the hostel alone, but then I remembered that he had been coping with his affliction on his own for years.

The following morning we both had been so anxious to get to the veranda of the New Stanley, where a day in Nairobi normally begins, that we started out an hour earlier than originally planned. Sheldon was supposed to come for me at ten, but when I went downstairs before nine, he was already waiting. He was beaming and boyish with a face as clear, fresh, and expressive as one might expect from a member of some heavenly hierarchy.

Over his jeans he wore a flowered shirt which was open to reveal his smooth, sexy chest, and to display many strands of beads. His multicolored hemp bag was slung over one shoulder. He never went anywhere without that shoulder bag, and I wondered why he was so attached to it. One thing I had to admit . . . whatever he chose to wear, he looked wonderfully attractive to me. Perhaps I wasn't becoming such a stuffy older lady after all.

Hand-in-hand we walked the few blocks through the shopping district of mainly Indian bazaars. In that part of town, the veranda of the New Stanley is the only place to rest out of the hot sun. It is roofed and open to the street on three sides to take advantage of any slight breeze. It is spacious, informal, and above all, inviting. Therefore it is almost always full of people. Sheldon and I looked at one another before entering and he squeezed my arm in a gesture of mutual understanding. We both were feeling a bit sentimental about being back.

At that hour of the morning there is a long buffet to one side of the serving area. The table is laid with enormous silver urns of coffee and tea, along with jugs of milk, bowls of sugar, and assortments of muffins, breads, and danish pastries.

About halfway inside we saw a large, unoccupied table meant for six, but it was the only one available so we decided to sit there. Sheldon asked me if I would prefer to order a full breakfast or have him bring some light snack from the buffet. I told him that I had been looking forward to a coffee and one of the special cheese danishes.

While I was waiting for Sheldon, I glanced around at the other tables. There seemed to be tourists from every corner of the globe and I played a guessing game to see if I could name the countries which were represented. I spotted several groups of suntanned, rugged looking people who must have been returning from safari. There were also a great many young people, whom Sheldon had described as "travel bums" like himself.

In turn people were looking at me with a curiosity which seemed similar to my own, and not at all like spectators regarding an actress in the flesh. Either they didn't recognize me or were considerate enough to allow me my privacy. I suspected that it was the former. That morning I had put on one of my most comfortable, well-worn safari suits along with a pair of desert boots. I had tied my hair back, and the canvas hat did a good job of concealing my blond ponytail as well as shading my face.

My attention was drawn to a plump girl in a wheelchair. She was being lifted in her chair up the steps of the veranda by a fellow and girl who fitted the description of travel bums. Certainly the very pretty blond holding one side of the metal frame did; she might have been on the road all her life by the look of her thread-bare jeans. She was tossing her straight blond hair and sharply thrusting her slim hips in an effort to lift the chair, making provoc-ative movements the way young women sometimes do when wishing to flaunt their sexuality. The man holding the other side of the chair was enormously big, rough-looking, and bearded. He was stifling a yawn, perhaps out of tiredness, but it appeared as though he were bored with the antics of the blond.

When they had settled the wheelchair onto the level of the porch they looked around for a table and then headed toward ours. The plump girl, who had now taken charge of wheeling herself by using her hands, arrived first and spoke to me: "Is it all right if we join you?"

I nodded in agreement, but the very big man had already sprawled on a chair opposite me, and the blond was noisily scrap-ing the chair next to mine from under the table.

The plump girl in the wheelchair asked me if I were traveling alone, and I told her no, that my companion was at the buffet table. Then she told me that she had been hitchhiking around Africa by herself for the last three months. I have never been able to imagine any woman hitchhiking and I certainly could not imagine a crippled woman traveling that way by herself across Africa. I'm sure I stared at her in complete amazement. And that was obviously the reaction she had been hoping for, because she all at once looked very proud of herself and pleased that she had been able to shock me.

"My name is Susan Kroner," she said. "I am from Munich."

She had a slight German accent but it hardly seemed noticeable. By the way she introduced herself, I gathered that it had become customary on the veranda of the New Stanley to give one's nationality along with one's name. I told her my name but she didn't seem to know me as an actress. Then I added, "The United States."

"Bert here is from the U.S." Susan said, smiling at the fellow. "Bert Mathews. He's a Vietnam War veteran."

Bert appeared to be scowling at me from under his heavy eyebrows, so that when I said, "How do you do," I fully expected him to sneer or growl in response. But he took me completely by surprise by being very gentle. He lumbered to his feet, removed his canvas hat, and shook my hand, taking care not to crush my fingers.

"Sorry, miss, if I seemed rude. It's just that we've been traveling all night and I haven't had a wink of sleep. I'm beat."

He had a drawl which was not fully southern and I guessed that he was from Maryland or Virginia, somewhere straddling the Mason-Dixon line. He went on to introduce the blond: "This here is Cathy Barr. She's French."

Cathy surprised me as well, because she shook my hand and greeted me in a manner that reminded me of someone with a finishing-school education. I think I had been prepared to dislike her, but I found her good manners and genuine smile disarming. She punched Bert playfully on the arm, turned to me again and said with a chuckle, "He is such a silly boy. Because I speak French, he tells everyone that I am French, but I am not. I am Swiss. I speak also German."

While Bert went for coffee, the girls told me a little about themselves. Cathy worked for a travel firm in Geneva and was at the moment taking advantage of a low-cost travel scheme which was one of the perquisites of her job.

Susan told me that she had been in a serious car crash three years before which had left her paralyzed from the waist down. She had decided that with her insurance money she was going to see the world.

The girls had met only ten days before when Susan had been hitchhiking on the road out of Dar es Salaam. She had been there along with a half-dozen other drifters who were leaving the port, but Cathy had spotted the girl in the wheelchair among them and told Bert to stop his camper truck. Cathy had said that anyone as brave as Susan deserved to be given a lift. Since their plans coincided, the three had decided to travel together and share expenses.

I gathered that even Bert and Cathy had not known one another for very long, but there seemed to be a strong bond of friendship among the three. It was an unmistakable devotion and one sensed it immediately. They were so completely different in appearance and background that their relationship appeared most unlikely. Perhaps for each it satisfied some deep emotional need and thus fostered a kind of dependence.

If Bert didn't qualify scientifically as a true giant, he certainly could not have been very far removed from that category. In addition, I suspected that in the southern United States he would have been considered "poor white trash." His experiences in Vietnam had undoubtedly set him apart even further, making it too difficult for him to go home again. I speculated that perhaps because of his size, he had never known female companionship while he was growing up. Now he had two young ladies sharing his camper truck and keeping him company on what would otherwise have been a lonely journey. Bert was perhaps a bit simple-minded, but his kindness seemed to know no bounds.

I imagined that Susan Kroner was from a working-class German family. Oddly enough, being in a wheelchair perhaps saved her from an otherwise inevitable future of drudgery and sameness. The insurance money had given her a passport to freedom and for her that seemed to outweigh the physical handicap. Certainly one never felt from Susan an ounce of jealousy or self-pity. She seemed to revel in Cathy's beauty and Bert's physical strength—in fact, she fairly glowed with admiration of them.

It was more difficult to speculate on an emotional history for the blond, lithe, well-educated Cathy. One got the impression of an affluent Swiss background, and perhaps some social standing. She had trained to be a travel agent because she adored travel. Possibly, since she was still quite young, the adventure for her was part of breaking away from the stifling limitations of a traditional background. Whatever, she appeared to cherish Bert and Susan for their own admirable qualities as adventurous individuals, giving generously of her affection as well.

Bert returned to the table with their coffee before Sheldon did with ours. Evidently Sheldon had run into some friends, and when I looked over he still seemed engrossed in conversation. Bert offered me his coffee but I assured him that I had had some earlier at the hotel and could wait for Sheldon to join us. Then he began telling me in detail about his late-model red-and-white camper, obviously the nicest thing he had ever owned.

"Yes, sir, she's a real beauty. Handles like a dream," he was saying. He suddenly paused and studied my expression, and I got the feeling that he wanted to apologize because he had such a beautiful camper and hadn't offered to share it with me. I found it touching when he said, "If you're heading north, miss, and you really need a ride, I think we could probably squeeze in two more people."

I thanked him, and told him that Sheldon and I wouldn't be traveling by car for another two weeks. The girls in particular seemed enthralled when I outlined our plans: Sheldon and I were to fly tomorrow morning by private plane to Tsavo in the south of Kenya for a two-day visit, then back to Nairobi to catch a commercial flight to the Seychelles for a ten-day visit before returning again to go on overland safari.

When I talked about Tsavo and the Seychelles the response I got from my new companions sent a thrill through me, the same thrill I always experienced when talking to the travel enthusiasts who congregated on the veranda of the New Stanley. It was the anticipation of that thrill, the unique experience of being accepted instantly as a member of the great family of adventurers that sent all of us rushing first thing every morning to join those already on the veranda. You shared your plans and experiences, and permitted that special excitement for travel to envelop you.

In turn I became thoroughly engrossed in listening to the plans Bert, Cathy, and Susan had made for the following two weeks. Perhaps I was being too impulsive, but I wanted to get together with these three at the end of that time so that we could exchange stories of our adventures. Without waiting to consult Sheldon, I promised them that we would meet again on the veranda in exactly two weeks' time.

Sheldon had left the buffet and was heading toward our table when a girl near the entrance shrieked and ran up to him. Lovingly she took hold of the multicolored hemp bag on Sheldon's shoulder and brought his attention to a similar one slung over her own. I heard them both saying "Katmandu." Cathy tossed her blond head and looked over at Sheldon with admiration. "Oh, he has been to Nepal!" she said excitedly. "Someday I must go there. I have seen the Himalayas from the Indian side but one day I must cross over."

So that was it, I thought to myself: that shoulder bag was the mark of someone special who had ventured to the other side of the Himalayas, and it could be worn like a medal of achievement to let others know that you were one of the far travelers who had actually been in Katmandu, Nepal.

Susan stretched forward in her wheelchair and asked me, "Is he your fellow?"

"Oh, wow!" Cathy said. "Is he?"

When I said "Yes," I said it with a feeling of considerable pride —and not a little relief that these young girls had referred to him as my fellow, and not my nephew—or heaven forbid, my son.

CHAPTER FOUR

On the morning of our second day in Africa we went to the section of the airport reserved for chartered flights, and when I saw the tiny plane that was waiting for us, my mouth went dry! I seldom consented to fly in private aircraft because the idea terrified me. I was further alarmed when I realized that of the three men we were talking to, our pilot was the boy who looked considerably younger than Sheldon. Nevertheless, as all was ready and the MacKennas had been kind enough to send their own plane for us, I steeled myself and climbed aboard.

Once we had taken off I had to admit that it was a lovely ride. I caught my image among clouds reflected in my side window and reminisced about my friendship with the MacKennas. I had met them first in 1964 when they had read that I was in the country filming and had sent me an open invitation to be their guest at

Tsavo Game Lodge. They had turned out to be lovely people, and I had always from that time on made a point of seeing them whenever I was in Kenya. At times they would come to Nairobi for a luncheon or dinner with me, and other times I would travel to Tsavo to visit them. My previous visits had always been day trips. This was to be the first time that I would be staying the night; two nights, in fact. I had asked the MacKennas for two single rooms, and now my only regret was that Sheldon and I again would be separated during the night. If we should decide in these next two days that we wanted to be together—well, I didn't feel that it would be possible while at Tsavo with my friends looking on.

It is a short flight of about thirty-five minutes to Tsavo. When we were ready to land there were hundreds, maybe even a thousand ostrich on the ground below us. It was an astonishing sight. They were galloping in circles, frightened by the noise of our plane. The ostrich were obliterating any clear view of the terrain's surface, and our boy pilot asked us which we thought looked like the dirt runway. Because of his youth one had to wonder about the extent of his flying experience, and now this youngster was asking us to play guess-where-we-should-land.

To the left we saw a moving funnel of dust heading toward the flock of ostrich. The pilot brought us in lower and we could see through the dust cloud that it was a Land Rover. The pilot told us the driver was Mr. MacKenna, or Mac, as everyone called him. The Land Rover stopped and Mac stood on the front seat, signaling with large straight arm movements to indicate the best path through the birds. We circled and climbed and then came in low, buzzing the ostrich along that path. Some of them were at least eight feet tall and must have weighed around three hundred pounds. They had the most peculiar run because their heads and bodies remained rigidly upright while their long, thin legs churned like the wheels of a locomotive.

34

Sheldon adored the sport of chasing the giant birds, and he and the boy pilot shouted with delight when the ostrich stampeded toward the horizon in front of us. I cringed, shut my eyes, and hoped that my stomach would soon stop crowding my chest. We leveled off and climbed, circling back the way we had come. Finally there was a clear dirt runway in front of us and we came in for a landing. It was a very bumpy landing but I felt greatly relieved when we bounced onto the rough, pock-marked earth.

As we taxied back toward the parked Land Rover I could see Mac leaning against the hood. He always made a broad, imposing figure, and today his elephant gun was slung over his shoulder as though it were a toy. He was wearing what I considered a glamorous safari suit because it was short-sleeved and belted, but his high boots were an ugly greenish-yellow rubber. Sheldon told me that those boots were the best protection in marshy land against things like snakebite, and that they in fact were called either "rhino" or "ugly" boots. They were as ugly as a rhino and as tough as its hide.

Even at a distance of perhaps a hundred yards, Mac's thick reddish-brown eyebrows and mustache gleamed in the sunlight. As we disembarked and walked toward him, the hazy distortion created by the bouncing heat waves made the mustache appear to rise to join his eyebrows, then fall again to rest on his upper lip.

I had almost forgotten what a loud, good-natured man Mac was. He roundly slapped both the pilot and Sheldon on their backs by way of a greeting. In his exuberance, I was afraid for a moment that he might forget himself and do the same to me. But when he raised his hand, it was to remove his pith helmet, releasing his bushy reddish-brown hair which looked impossible to control. Mac always reminded me of one of those daredevil explorers straight out of a nineteenth-century print.

As he opened the door for me, I could see that the rear seat of his jeep was covered with a rubber ground cloth that was full of blood and heaped with a variety of carcasses. Among this display of mayhem and slaughter I could make out a legless zebra, several smaller skinned animals, and a deer with its antlers torn out. It was absolutely sickening and the sight made me nauseous. Not wanting to be impolite, I nevertheless climbed into the front seat beside our host. Sheldon got on the running board and clung to the side. The pilot, who was carrying our luggage, began walking the short distance to the lodge.

"Mac, I thought hunting was forbidden on these game reserves," Sheldon said as a statement rather than an accusation.

"Depends on what you're hunting," Mac said. "See this badge? I'm not only an innkeeper, I'm also a government-appointed ranger. I hunt poachers."

"You mean you hunt men?" I said in horror. "But Mac, I can't believe that you would hunt men . . . and with guns!"

"Yes," he replied in a fury, "I hunt men . . . the great, greedy destroyers. And I hunt them with guns. They have more defenses than the animals have."

He had become so impassioned that I thought it would be wise to let the subject drop, but Mac had more to say and he was determined to say it: "You see those carcasses in the back? I had to kill them . . . to put them out of their misery. Horrible schemes these poachers come up with . . . spiked traps or barbed wires to snare them, while they cut off the tusks or horns or feet. They don't care if the poor creatures lie there suffering for hours on end before death comes. Well, that's part of my job, too, to put the poor things out of their misery. And if I witness the bastards who are causing that misery, I'll shoot them or even cut off their ba . . ." He caught himself before saying *balls* in front of a lady and, at any rate, we had arrived at the rear of the lodge.

He braked but made no move to leave the jeep, and he continued speaking but now in a more cheerful tone: "Of course, sometimes that's how we get our fresh meat here at the lodge. I came across a wounded kudo bull a few days back. A huge fellow about six hundred pounds or so. I had to shoot him. With the help of some of my boys, we skinned, cleaned and hung him. Good venison meat that is . . . we thought as a special treat we'd serve the kudo for dinner tonight."

I reflected on all the blood and flesh just behind me in the back of the jeep and really wished that he hadn't identified what we were going to have for dinner. I was also thankful that we wouldn't be staying long enough for the carnage behind me to have been hung and ready in time for our meals.

It's funny but if you are a city dweller, you might eat meat all your life without ever thinking about its origin. When I walk into a butcher shop, I avoid looking at sides or legs or ribs or any distinctive pieces that remind me of the fact that I'm actually planning to eat a dead animal. In fact I prefer the supermarket cases where I am not obliged to see anything on display but neat little, nearly unidentifiable packages.

Mac was saying, "It's almost ten o'clock. No sense going out on the reserve now. Soon it will be too hot. The hottest part of the day is from eleven until around two. I suggest I get someone to show you to your rooms. Then when you've unpacked, come to the terrace, say hello to Sally, and have a nice cool drink with us. You'll find that we do everything early here. Lunch is at twelve sharp and then most people take a nap because they have been up for breakfast at five. I'll take you out in the Land Rover myself when the sun begins to set. Those are the best times to see the animals . . . at sunrise or sunset. I'll give you the full guided tour. You'll have a view that most people never get."

The lodge was like coming upon a stone platform in the wilderness, or an open railroad station with no tracks. It was a long, squat construction built of jagged rock. The platform was flat, tiled in flagstone and made into one gigantic terrace. It was partially protected from the elements by an awning made of thatch and a thatched screen that ran along the rear wall of the building, hiding the unpicturesque sight of trash cans and parked vehicles. The terrace was the place where every communal activity of the lodge took place, from the serving of drinks and meals to relaxing, socializing, and animal-watching.

The guest rooms were on the ground level underneath the terrace and seemed to be built there as an afterthought. They were narrow, uniform, and little more than cubbyholes with a view. Each was furnished with a wooden bed covered in a canopy of mosquito netting, a few shelves but no hanging closet, and a tiny toilet and shower enclosed by an opaque plastic curtain.

The room had two doors: a sturdy back door which locked with a key, and a flimsy screen door which was only held by a latch. You entered your room through the sturdy door which was located on the rear side of the building. Once inside and past the bathroom facility, you faced the screen door and a window which gave you light and a view, the same view of spacious bush country as you had from the front of the terrace. The screen door opened onto a long, narrow porch which ran the length of the ground level and was roofed by the overhang of the terrace above. Sheldon and I opened our screen doors and stepped onto the porch at approximately the same time. We doubled up in laughter as we waved to one another from the length of the porch. Sheldon's room was at one end of the lodge and mine at the other.

The literature in the room informed guests about the activities and routine of the lodge. Animal-watching was best early in the morning and late at night, when the animals were most likely to come to the salt lick which had been planted nearby as a lure. It warned guests of the early meal hours, and stated that those wishing to animal-watch at night were to bring their own flashlights for getting to and from their rooms. The floodlight illuminating the area around the salt lick had its own mini-generator and burned all night, but the main generator which provided the electricity to the lodge was shut down at precisely ten P.M.

There was also a warning in bold letters about not getting too close to the animals:

DO NOT TAKE A WALK!
DO NOT LEAVE YOUR CAR WHEN DRIVING IN THE RE-SERVE!
DO NOT OPEN YOUR CAR WINDOWS!
DO NOT TORMENT THE ANIMALS!
DO NOT CHASE THE LARGE ANIMALS WITH YOUR CAR OR THEY MAY ATTACK!
DO NOT LEAVE THE LODGE AT NIGHT!
DO NOT ROAM THE GROUNDS OF THE LODGE TO GO ANYWHERE BUT TO YOUR CAR OR THE TERRACE ABOVE!
DO NOT OPEN YOUR ROOM WINDOW!
DO NOT LEAVE YOUR SCREEN DOOR UNLOCKED!

I thought the last one was strange: the door was flimsy and the lock was only a crude latch.

After I had freshened up, I left my room by the sturdy rear door. It was just a few paces from my room to the stone steps at the side of the building, and I climbed them to the terrace.

As one stepped onto it there was a bamboo bar to one side, dining tables set for lunch in the center section under the thatched awning, and at the far end some lounging chairs placed to overlook the area of the salt lick. The edge of the terrace had a three-foot-high stone guardrail, and set along it were a dozen or so small garden tables, each with its own umbrella. The peculiar thing I noticed (which I had not noticed on other visits) was that each table had on it an ashtray full of pebbles and a slingshot.

I had felt certain that the terrace was deserted, but the moment I sat down at one of the small tables by the railing an African materialized from behind the bamboo bar and came for my order.

He was wearing a khaki uniform and carrying a tray with a dish of peanuts. I heard a strange chattering and, turning, saw that three large, olive-brown baboons had appeared on the other end of the terrace. They were hurrying along the top of the stone railing in my direction as if we had an appointment and they were late. It was surprising and so funny that I laughed out loud. I turned to say something about them to the waiter just in time to see him lift the slingshot from my table, load it with a pebble, and shoot it at the baboons. They screamed and raced to the far end of the railing. Then once they were completely out of harm's way, they challenged him by posturing with their chests thrown out and their tails arched. They were still waving their arms and scolding the waiter when Sheldon emerged from the stairwell.

I had ordered us each a gin-and-tonic, and when the waiter had gone back to the bar, the baboons cautiously began to work their way back toward our table. They were making a great pretense of being otherwise occupied and deliberately walking backwards in order to deceive us into thinking that they were not advancing.

Sheldon sat down, still wet from his shower. His hair was slicked back with the water, and droplets of it trickled onto the collar of his fresh shirt. I had placed myself completely under the protection of the umbrella but he pulled his chair away from the table and stretched out in the sun.

His shirt was only buttoned once, near the waist, exposing taut skin, glistening with fine golden hairs beneath his assortment of beads. "You should be dry in a matter of seconds in this heat," I said. "What took you so long?"

"This is one of my three daytime shirts, so I took the time to wash the other two."

"But," I protested, "you could have gotten your laundry done here at the lodge, I'm sure."

With a twinkle in his eye he said, "I have my servants to take care of everything when I'm in Spain. I showed you the photograph, didn't I, of them carrying me on an oriental carpet up the circular staircase of the castle? When I travel I make it a point to be self-sufficient."

Then he signaled me with his eyes and lowered his hand several times in a slight bounce indicating that I should stay put. He whispered, "Now, my darling, if you want to be amused don't move for a moment . . . but out of the corner of your eye, observe the peanut dish."

I did so and saw some clever thieving: slowly and noiselessly two shiny fingers with long sharp nails were extracting peanuts from the dish one by one.

I couldn't resist looking directly at the baboon. Because of the large, brightly colored swelling of the genital region, I knew that it was a female. Although her long snout with its nostrils at the tip made her look monstrous, there was such an intelligence in those liquid eyes that I felt a sympathy for her. I took several peanuts from the dish and made an offering. The baboon bared her teeth threateningly and I froze.

There was a deep, terrifying growl to the side of me, and both the baboon and I jumped in fright. She flung herself over the railing . . . I whipped around in the direction of the sound. Sheldon had transformed his face into an expression like a wild beast's, not unlike that of a wolf. It was grotesque and I found myself cringing from him, but what an extraordinary intuitive power he had displayed. I felt that the baboon was about to bite and his action had saved me.

He softened and became himself once more. Leaning over he stroked my arm and said gently, "Sorry, my darling, there seemed to be no time to help in any other way. She had to be warned off because I was afraid that she was about to rip away your finger."

I was quiet for a time and sat catching my breath, wondering at the speed with which tragedy might occur, even on a bright sunlit terrace where you might least expect it. Of course this was a continent where one was forced into becoming acutely aware of a moment-to-moment survival code.

The waiter brought our gin-and-tonics but Sheldon declined his and asked instead for a soft drink. Rather than turning the extra drink away, I asked the waiter to leave it for me. I was only too happy to accept a double gin at the moment.

Sheldon explained, "I have to be careful because of my medication not to drink too much alcohol. A glass of wine now and then is about all I can allow myself."

I said, "Sheldon, tell me, why should that baboon have attacked me? I haven't always found them to be treacherous."

"Not always. But sometimes a female baboon, particularly in her menstrual period, will attack and even kill another female primate, of whatever species." He smiled at me and added, "We of course are primates. I'm sure the slingshots are here mostly because these baboons have become terrible pests. But they do have powerful limbs and those enormous canine teeth, as you saw. They can be extremely dangerous, especially since they associate in such large troops."

I noticed that I had subconsciously placed the slingshot closer to my right hand and while toying with it, had loaded it with a big pebble.

Just then we saw in the distance a minibus and two cars heading toward the lodge. It was eleven o'clock and the guests were returning to freshen up and have a drink before lunch.

We heard a man coming up the stairs and the loud voice was unmistakably Mac's. He entered followed by a large woman carrying a tiny vase of flowers. It was Sally.

Sally was a tall, buxom, ruddy-looking woman of about fifty-five or sixty. Her blond hair, streaked with gray, was pulled tightly back in a ponytail which emphasized the broadness of her rosy face, just as did the crisp white blouse she was wearing above her full gingham skirt. Her feet were encased in sensible oxfords, and she walked toward us with as purposeful a stride as her husband's. I rose to greet her and still she towered over me.

"I'm so delighted that we are finally going to have the pleasure of your company for a couple of days," she said, clasping my hand and kissing me on the cheek. She carefully placed in my hand a tiny vase containing one purple and one crimson cyclamen. "These beautiful little flowers are for you. You have no idea how precious they are in this part of the country. Here, we learn to live without most of the sweetnesses of refined life." And it was odd and touching coming from such a sturdy-looking woman as Sally.

CHAPTER FIVE

Sally MacKenna was a marvelous hostess with the ability to make one feel welcome and a gift for bringing together people who proved to be excellent company for one another. I watched her transform a terrace of strangers into groups of socially compatible luncheon parties.

Sally and Mac did not stay on the terrace for lunch. For them, the working day at the lodge began at three-thirty in the morning, so they took advantage of the heat-induced lull during the middle of the day to catch up on their rest. After having arranged a table with a view for us, Sally excused herself until teatime. She had introduced us to a couple from Vancouver, Ann and Dick Fraser, whom within minutes we found to be bright, energetic, and sparkling good company.

Ann and Dick Fraser were professional photographers, tops in their field and dedicated to their work. They were in their late thirties or early forties. Although married for twenty years they had no children, preferring instead to devote themselves to a career. Ann and Dick were thin, wiry people who looked more like twins than husband and wife. Ann's short, fringed brown hair was almost identical to Dick's, and from the back, dressed in safari suits, one was hard pressed to tell them apart. They both chain-smoked. Hung around their necks along with the light meters and cameras were cigarettes in a leather box and a lighter in a pouch on a long leather thong. As we talked, I observed the dexterity with which they used all their gadgets. Their hands seemed constantly to be moving between one object or another, yet their conversation was never interrupted by it.

There was a more or less fixed menu. Meals were included in the price of the room, but drinks, which were of wide variety, were charged separately. The MacKennas were known in East Africa for their exceptional wine cellar, particularly in a climate considered hostile to the preservation of wine. Generously, Mac had provided us with a complimentary bottle of French rosé, which was chilled to perfection and brought to our table in a silver champagne bucket. We were served a chunky country-style paté followed by an extra-rich game pie; not a meal for anyone with a tendency toward gout. Fresh vegetables were in short supply but as the meal cried out for a salad the chef had cleverly devised one of cold cooked vegetables in vinaigrette dressing, arranged on a thin wedge of lime Jello as a replacement for lettuce.

While after lunch most of the guests retired from the terrace to their rooms, Ann, Dick, Sheldon, and I remained. We made ourselves comfortable in lounge chairs which had been moved under the thatched awning where we might reap the protection of its shade. We had footstools for added comfort, and Ann and Dick each had an ashtray to accommodate their chain-smoking. (There would be no smoking once we were out on the reserve. I remembered that as one of Mac's most strictly enforced rules.) Along with our coffee, we had ordered a thermos of iced lemonade and some glasses to be placed on a table near us, in anticipation of those thirsty hours while the waiters took their well-deserved siestas and there would be no service.

Once there was no longer any human activity to speak of, the baboons descended in large troops. So did bands of red guenon monkeys. The guenons had brick-red hair, long slender bodies about the size of domesticated cats, long legs and tails, and short black faces.

Except for the large, heavy, or anchored objects, everything on the terrace had been removed for safety. Between the baboons and guenons, they made short work of stealing all objects which proved liftable. At one moment I wiped my forehead and let my arm slip to my side with my handkerchief dangling. Before I realized, it had been snatched by a guenon. Dick, despite having a cigarette in his mouth, swiftly lifted his camera and captured the entire scene from the theft, to my startled expression, to the monkey standing a few feet away waving my handkerchief and grimacing at me.

Ann and Dick, whom Sheldon and I were to come to think of as the Fraser twins, were in East Africa on assignment for the third time in as many years. They had become experts on the local wildlife. They told us that baboons were common to Tsavo. Baboons are terrestrial and inhabit open country. But it is rare to see monkeys in such a place, as they are arboreal. Red guenons are one of the only breed of monkey not entirely arboreal in habit, and thus found in sparsely wooded country such as the savannah around us. It was, however, most unusual to see monkeys and baboons running together.

Two enormous male baboons were taking a special interest in Sheldon on account of his multicolored beads. At first he shot pebbles at them, but they kept coming back, circling him in an ominous way. I felt some of them must weigh as much as eighty or ninety pounds, and I was apprehensive of them creeping in to grab the beads and injuring Sheldon in the process, So for my sake he buttoned his shirt front over the beads and allowed me to further conceal the jewelry by tying my scarf around his neck.

Ann and Dick fished ice cubes from the thermos and threw them on the flagstones, thinking they might get some amusing photographs of the monkeys playing with the cold toys. But a nasty fight seemed to be brewing between the two species for possession of the ice.

Considering the formidable size of the baboons, the guenons were amazingly brave. Ann told us that baboons often tore to pieces creatures the size of the monkeys. Dick contended that in this instance both groups were bluffing by making threatening sounds. Nevertheless, we all were relieved when the ice melted. For me, the funniest sight was of the baboons and monkeys closest to the melting cubes who kept dipping their fingers into the little pools of water and puzzling over the metamorphosis.

We talked to Ann and Dick about the photographing of animals until a drowsiness overtook us. Then we attempted to do some reading, but everyone finally gave in to the fierce afternoon heat by dozing.

It was after tea, at about five-thirty, when we set out to view the reserve. Ann and Dick had their own Land Rover, the back seat of which was cluttered with photographic equipment. Sheldon and I rode with Mac, who had brought along in his jeep an African tracker named Kitua. The black tracker spoke only Swahili, was dressed in the same sort of safari suit as Mac's, and he too sported a ranger badge. He was seated in the front passenger seat, holding both his own trim Springfield and Mac's ungainly elephant gun. Sheldon and I were in the back seat from where the rubber ground cloth, together with its carcasses, had been removed. Sally Mac-

Kenna had loaned us each a pair of binoculars, and Sheldon had a compact camera in his Katmandu shoulder bag.

I think because of my previous experiences, as well as the many descriptions I have read about the special feeling one gets when witnessing wild animals in their natural habitat, I had expected a leisurely drive through the game reserve which would lead me once again to that slow, poetic discovery of the natural state of things. But I had forgotten what Mac was like behind the wheel, and I had not reckoned on the manic dedication of professional photographers like the Frasers.

There was great excitement plus an urgency to get started. It had been reported to Mac that a pride of lions had been spotted making a kill. We absolutely tore out of the parking lot. With the Fraser's Land Rover close on our tail, we bounced and sometimes flew over the savannah. The object was to get to the sight of the kill as quickly as possible. With one hand I held the binoculars (which were on a strap around my neck) away from my body to keep them from thumping my chest, and with the other hand I fought to keep myself on the seat and inside the jeep. Sheldon was seated on the trunk. For balance, his feet were on the seat and his arms stretched in a pyramid brace. He seemed elated by the speed and the force of the breeze sweeping over us. When he saw me holding on so tightly he laughed, motioning for me to join him on the trunk.

I looked around at the Frasers. Ann not only was standing up in the front, but stretching over to the back seat to reload her camera. The Frasers were leaner and harder of muscle than I, but I knew them to be about my age. Ann looked so strong and capable. She looked the way most women have at one time or another fantasized about looking. What the hell . . . I threw caution to the wind and stood up. Once standing, I found it a less jarring ride and easier to keep my equilibrium. Mainly it was great fun. When Sheldon saw my daring stance, he reached over and gave me a big hug.

We continued to drive at great speed, and when I finally saw the lovely sight of giraffes nibbling acacia trees and impalas doing graceful leaps, my eyes were watering so much that it was like watching an out-of-focus, jerky projection of a home movie.

Mac raised his hand, indicating to the Frasers that he was about to stop. Dick Fraser pulled up beside us.

Mac said, "We've been traveling in the general direction where the lions were spotted. Now it's up to Kitua to tell me where to head from here."

Kitua had gotten out and was observing something in the distance. Then he got down on all fours and buried his face in the grass. After having taken a series of photographs of Kitua in that odd pose, Dick asked, "What the hell is he doing?"

"He's smelling for them," Mac replied. "He's the best tracker we have. Even when there are no discernible tracks, Kitua can smell his way to a lion."

Kitua's smelling was a serious ritual and demanded several minutes of strict concentration on his part, and respectful attention on ours. Still on all fours, he lifted his face from the grass and directed his nostrils first one way and then another. Mac told us that once Kitua caught the scent, he would be able to follow the line of it and the direction in which it traveled. Kitua stopped, his head motionless and fixed on a direction. Then lowering himself close to the ground again, he crawled rapidly forward in a geometrically straight line. Suddenly he lifted his arm, pointing to the horizon with a strong motion. He looked at us triumphantly.

"That's it!" Mac yelled, "Let's go!"

Kitua dashed back to the jeep and we again were off like a bucking bronco. Kitua stood. He seemed to be sniffing the air. Perhaps he was struggling to keep the scent. He and Mac were continuously indicating directions with their hands. Then Mac slowed to a crawl and motioned for the Frasers to come up beside us. "We have to choose at this point," Mac shouted. "Kitua says that the lions have finished eating and left the kill. What do you want to photograph first, the remains of the kill or the lions digesting their meal?"

The Frasers opted for the remains of the kill. Just over the next thorny incline we saw vultures circling, and below us in the valley hyenas were tearing at a wildebeest carcass. After having located the kill Mac did not advance any nearer and Sheldon did not indicate that he wished to photograph the scene. But the Frasers drove down the hill and stopped in close proximity to the carcass. They were frantically snapping their pictures, changing lenses, changing cameras, and changing film, all in seemingly nonstop motion. I couldn't imagine what they found of photographic interest, unless perhaps it was the fight ensuing among the scavengers.

The Frasers' lust for gory pictures having been satisfied, we continued on our way to the watering hole where Kitua said we would find the lions resting. Perhaps a mile before we reached them, every one of us could smell the lions, or rather their digestive process. The fumes of their stomach acid rendering the huge quantity of meat they had consumed was the vilest of smells. That odor of decaying flesh is instantly recognizable, even when smelled for the first time.

The big cats, a male and two females, were wallowing in the mud alongside the watering hole. Their eyes were glazed and they looked drugged from the recent gorging. With enormous swollen stomachs, they lay in sated agony. They kept rolling from side to side every few minutes, trying to place their distended guts in some more comfortable position. Whether lying on their bellies, their sides, or on their backs with their paws in the air, they kept their jaws stretched wide as if yawning. As they ventilated through their open mouths, the smell of raw meat digesting accompanied by the odor of copious farts exploding in recurrent blasts was repulsive almost beyond compare.

We were safe in our open jeep because gasoline fumes disguise the human odor. But these lions were so full of food, we felt had we walked up to them out of reach of those playful paws, we still would have been perfectly safe.

When we decided to return for the evening, the sun was setting and the western sky was breathtakingly beautiful. The savannah was now pink, dotted by a golden thorn. It was a picture to be savored, but Mac tore back to the lodge at the same rate as he had set out. Far from enjoying the ride, we almost ran over a family of warthogs. They were lined up according to size, trotting along with the proud papa in the lead, the tiniest piggy bringing up the rear. We loomed upon them suddenly and they scattered with terrible squeals. Fortunately Mac was able to brake in time and we only shattered their dignity, not their porcine bodies.

Warthogs are the funniest creatures in the bush. Top-heavy little pigs with a lion's mane and huge tusks at their front end, their hindquarters are shamefully bare and puny. Their tails rise bolt upright in a ridiculous salute when they are startled, expressing surprise.

We started up again, but I turned and watched them as they quickly regrouped and trotted into the scrub, disappearing further down the track. Behind me, silhouetted on a distant hill, there was a magnificent creature poised like a lonely sentry. He was a truly noble beast with fine spiraling horns. I was much distressed to learn that he was a kudo bull. Kudo was on tonight's menu.

When we gathered once again at cocktail hour with the Frasers and the MacKennas, Sheldon had one of his fierce headaches, attributable to his epilepsy. These headaches came on without prior warning and caused him great suffering. He had taken six or eight aspirin and when they had failed to control the pain, I insisted that he go to bed early. It was a stroke of bad luck for me that his headache developed when it did. I feel that if he had been with me, I would have been spared the danger which I faced later that night and my first night at Tsavo might not have been one of sheer terror.

I hadn't been able to face the slab of black kudo meat on my plate. I'd toyed with the maize (which had been smothered in thick gravy) and the strange green bananas (which had been flown in from the Congo and which were dry and piquant), so I had eaten almost nothing at all. That would have been all right if I hadn't had glass after glass of strong red wine during the meal and endless refills of port afterwards. Without so much to drink on an empty stomach, I might have kept my wits about me. As it was, I stayed on the terrace talking to the MacKennas and the Frasers until nearly midnight, all of us ignoring the usual ten o'clock curfew. Even when elephants came to the salt lick that night, I failed to observe them.

Once we had called it a night, I held to the stone railing and took each step down, one by one. Five or six times I tried before managing to get my key into the keyhole. I came into the room, threw some cold water on my face, and was drying it when the lights began to fade. Even in my alcoholic stupor I remembered about the generator shutting down. I had no flashlight and no matches. In the last vestiges of fading light I ran and got into bed, tucking the mosquito netting securely around the mattress. While still able to see, my main concern was to not get more mosquito bites added to the numerous ones I already had received on the terrace. Getting undressed, I threw my clothes on top of the covers. By that time I was in total darkness.

I had just closed my eyes when I heard the chatter of baboons. There must have been hundreds, traveling the length of the porch, coming in my direction. They were getting closer and louder. I turned my head to look. The screen door. I froze, unable to breathe. The screen door! Was the screen door locked? I had stepped out onto the porch that morning and waved at Sheldon. Had I relocked the screen door? Sometimes they tore creatures to bits with their powerful fingers and teeth. Sometimes females attacked other female primates. My God! Was the latch on the screen door? Was there time to check it? No! No time to get out of bed. No time to get my hand on the lock. No time to get out the back door. I didn't dare move. They were nearly there, and I was trapped. They would kill me before my screams could summon help. There was no time to save myself. That door was either locked or unlocked. Therein rested my fate.

I was sweating, yet cold. Then I could see grotesque shapes swarming around my window and door. Ugly snouts protruding into small spaces. Protruding into every square inch of flimsy covering on that screen door. I could smell them, which meant that they could smell me. If I could see them, then they could see me. Some growled. Some barked hoarsely. All were threatening. As I became more and more terrified, they got more and more excited.

Then I heard that tiny sound. That tiny, all important sound. That sound I had been listening for. I heard it despite the terrible chattering. The latch sound. One had tried the latch. I heard the door begin to move outwards. Time seemed to stop. I was numb. I was in that merciful state of shock which closes off the full impact of horror, prepared for the onslaught.

It had happened in a fraction of a second . . . in the next second after I heard the door begin to move . . . I heard the click. The life-saving click of the latch. Then those sounds repeated but faster and faster as insistent baboons tugged at the handle of the screen door and it clicked back to its locked position: Out-click, out-click, out-click. And on and on until they got tired and reluctantly turned to moved on. I lay there listening to them as they moved further and further into the distance. For hours in a half-dazed nightmare, I heard them traveling in my dreams.

ABOVE: Lions wallowed in the mud beside a watering hole after the kill. The fumes of their stomach acid digesting the wildebeest they'd consumed smelled terribly.

BELOW: I wasn't as worried about taking this photo of the giraffes as I was photographing the lions, even if it was after the kill.

A typical game lodge terrace, with a stone wall encompassing it to help ward off unwanted "guests."

ABOVE: These baboons look harmless, but they're much larger—and dangerous—than they appear in this photo. They regularly descend upon the patio at Tsavo Lodge, which is why each table comes equipped with a slingshot and ashtray full of pebbles. *Photo credit: Enrico Mandel-Mantello*

BELOW: We sighted this kudo from the patio of the Tsavo Lodge. I was upset to learn that kudo was on the menu that night. *Photo credit: Enrico Mandel-Mantello*

ABOVE: A lion showing what he thought of us. *Photo credit: Enrico Mandel-Mantello*

BELOW: Diners get in line for their meal. You can see vultures waiting in the not-too-distant background. *Photo credit: Enrico Mandel-Mantello*

CHAPTER SIX

I was stirred to semiconsciousness by the brightness of the room. Everything had been very cold, but finally I was warm in the bed. I felt very tired, almost drained. My thinking was hazy. I was aware that I wasn't at home, that it wasn't my bed, but I couldn't think what Italian city I was in. Rolling slowly onto my back, it took a few minutes for me to will myself to open my eyes. My left eye seemed to be sealed with sleep. My right one opened slightly. "Oh, God, I'm imprisoned in a spider's web!" I thought, because through a blur of brightness, I saw directly over me the bulbous underbelly of a large grayish spider.

The hideous arachnid seemed to be palpating the gossamer threads of the web, floating over and surrounding me.

It was my fear that jolted me awake. Then I remembered that the covering, which was fairly shimmering in the first sunbeams and appeared to be floating on rays of light filtering through the window, was in fact a mosquito netting. It covered my bed completely from the canopy at the top to the underside of the mattress, protecting me from the spider. There was a screen door . . . the screen door which had protected me from ferocious night intruders. How could I have forgotten I was in Tsavo? What was Sheldon doing at this moment? I wondered.

We had arrived in Africa, in Kenya, three days ago; now we were at Tsavo. It was January 1971, I wasn't sure which day, but the Cartier traveling clock, which I had gotten from my children by post for Christmas, was on the bedside table and it read five A.M. As for the time difference in L.A. or Rome; that was too difficult before breakfast. Oh, no, I was probably already late for breakfast, I thought. Well, I'd had a bad shock last night.

I tried to sit up but my head hurt. Why was I naked? Oh, yes, I had thrown off my clothes in a hurry. My mouth was parched and I needed a cup of coffee. Perhaps my headache was a hangover. Perhaps it was a combination of the alcohol and the shock.

There was a tap at the door. I called, "Yes?" A key turned. I hadn't meant for anyone to enter. I was naked. I sat up straight, pulling the covers up to my chest. The door opened and an African waiter entered with a steaming mug of tea. He carried it to the bed, and I eagerly raised the mosquito netting and accepted it. I should have asked him to remove the spider but I desperately wanted the tea first. Just as suddenly he was gone. I normally drank coffee in the mornings, but this British-style tea was wonderful; a brewed, full-bodied tea with milk—more thirst-quenching than coffee.

I drank every drop of the tea and watched the spider inching its way slowly down toward my feet. Was there some way to ring for another tea? Should I call for someone to come and remove the spider? Yes, I'd have to or I'd be afraid to come back into the room —but remove it, not kill it. This was Africa, and you couldn't kill them all. You had to learn to live with other creatures, but also to learn to be extremely careful and not let your guard down. You had to relearn the art of survival, which years of a false sense of security in a man-made environment had obliterated. You had to recall your ancestral instincts. You had to learn to survive.

Our last hours at Tsavo were a time as good as lost to me because of the blinding headache I had to battle. The Frasers had flown out by the first light, so I hadn't had a chance to say good-bye to them. Sheldon, whose own headache had disappeared by morning, had arisen early enough to help them and the boy pilot load the private plane with their cases of photographic equipment. And Sheldon had gotten for us a copy of Ann and Dick's itinerary. It was possible that we might run into them again; at least we were hoping to.

Nor had I seen any animals to speak of that day, because I wasn't feeling well enough to tear around the countryside with Mac. It was Sheldon who eagerly set out on the chase with our host. I'd had a suspicion that they were going to have a better time without me. Later I discovered that they had gone scouting for traps and poachers, but at the time I didn't want to know a thing about it. That day I was happier simply relaxing in the shade with pitcher after pitcher of lemonade. It was nice for me that Sally MacKenna had taken time off from her multitude of responsibilities so that we could have a long conversation. I enjoyed Sally's company and had always hoped for an opportunity to get to know her better.

That evening I retired before Sheldon did. We were to be awakened at four A.M. and the boy pilot was to have the plane ready for a five A.M. takeoff, because we were due to catch a connecting flight to the Seychelle Islands that same morning.

When I awakened I felt like myself again and Sheldon, too, was feeling splendid. To celebrate, we each ordered the full, hearty English breakfast of fried eggs, sausages, grilled mushrooms, stewed tomatoes, fried bread, and strong black tea.

It seemed we could speak of nothing but having missed one another the day before. Nor could we resist touching one another or secretly holding hands through breakfast. Occasionally, when no one was looking, we stole a fleeting kiss. Because I had been cautious, we hadn't actually kissed before, but today we were behaving like coy, flirtatious teenagers. Perhaps it was because we were on our way to what travel experts called the most beautiful islands in the world and the French referred to as the Islands of Love . . . but perhaps it was because we felt that tingling expectancy that we were about to make love.

In less than two hours after takeoff in the private single-propeller plane, we were seated on the commercial twin-propeller plane on our way to Mahé. In another two hours Sheldon and I, along with six other passengers, were landing at the first International Airport of Mahé.

Although they already were calling it the new airport, the expansion was not as yet completed. The old runway on which we were obliged to land was only just long enough for our plane. On the first run the pilot misjudged the distance. He touched the wheels down briefly, then climbed steeply and brought us in again, fast and sharp like a combat landing.

As we disembarked, a police band in white uniform was playing in our honor, and the man appointed governor of the republic within the commonwealth was there in person to greet us. Sheldon and I looked around thinking perhaps one of our fellow passengers was a head of state, but not so. Eight tourists at one time was sufficient cause for great excitement on Mahé, and the big twin-propeller commercial plane had landed thus far only a dozen times at the new, if incomplete, airport. A large crowd of natives had gathered in anticipation of our arrival, as had almost all the representatives of the government, including the governor himself.

The trip to the Seychelles had been Sheldon's idea. And I thought that he was quite right in wanting to come early on in the history of the International Airport. Surely it would only be a question of time before this charming custom of meeting aircraft was a thing of the past. All too soon the Seychellois would come to take airplanes for granted once the jumbo jets roared in on a regular basis, even irritated by the multitude of tourists crowding the islands. But on this day the governor shook hands with each of us and personally presented us with handpainted maps of the islands. Mahé, with its fifty-five square miles, was by far the largest one pictured, and a scale at one corner showed that it was seventeen miles long, between three and five miles wide, and the mountain range down its center was from two thousand to three thousand feet high.

As yet, no bus service was available from the airport and Mahé had only two taxicabs, so passengers were requested to wait their turn for transportation to their living accommodations. Those who were last in line, however, were compensated by having more time to spend over coffee with the government officials, as well as with the most gracious and erudite governor. Sheldon and I deliberately hung back when, in answer to our questions, the governor embarked on a short summary of the islands: apparently they numbered around one hundred, but some were little more than rocks in the ocean. The Seychelles were thought to be the tops of mountains left when Africa split from Asia during the Ice Age, since they were composed of the hardest and oldest hornblende granite known to man—about six hundred million years old.

He told us that Mahé, of course, had the largest population, but that only four out of all the islands were inhabited. Not, it seemed, because they were uninhabitable, but because there were so few settlers, plus the fact that the expansive coral reef was low-lying and subsequently cut off access to a great many islands for days at a time during low tide.

The governor made us all laugh when he said, "Don't think for one moment, please, that we have misspelled *sea shells*. The Seychelles were named in honor of Vicomte Sechelles, controller general of finance to Louis XV."

"Then they were originally French?" I asked.

"Yes, but they were ceded to Britain by the Treaty of Paris in 1814, and jolly good luck for us. As well as the *Iles D'amour,* our islands have been called the *Pearls of the Indian Ocean,* and General Gordon of Khartoum fame even went so far as to declare them to be the original *Garden of Eden.*"

The governor went on to tell us that the islands could be described as paradise because they were never struck by cyclones, typhoons, hurricanes, or tidal waves. There had never been a shark incident. There were no snakes, no dangerous animals, and one was even hard pressed to see an insect of any type.

We thanked the governor and accepted his invitation to tea at Government House sometime during our stay. One of the taxis then became available and Sheldon told the driver we were going to Frau Kupferman's house at North Point. She was a German widow who ran what was reported to be the best and cleanest guest house on the islands.

We were hoping to have a look at the islands' only city, and as it happened Victoria was on the east coast of Mahé, halfway between the airport and the North Point. An impressive new highway had been built from the airport into Victoria; before long it rose sharply and soon we were climbing high above the sea. From that considerable height and because of the absolute clarity of the air and sea, we had a wonderful view of the inlying islands of Cerf and St. Ann. We also could see quite distinctly miles of coral reef barely under the water's surface and dozens of tiny islands which dotted the horizon.

Then we descended into Victoria, a port city famous in shipping circles for its deep harbor. Leading off the harbor were narrow streets and open-air markets. The central part of the city, without a single modern building, looked as it must have a century before.

At its heart there was a miniature tower clock, a replica of those larger ones found in Great Britain. A statue of Queen Victoria stood atop a fountain in the park as if surveying her city.

Outside Victoria the road again climbed into the mountains and since the island was very narrow at this point, we were able to view the sea on either side of us. When the taxi stopped at our address, we got out beside a picket fence at a gate on the highway. The white framed colonial house was isolated on the ridge above us, and we felt certain that its vista through the tall trees of the North Point must be extraordinary.

There were steep stone steps leading up to the front porch and the picket fence enclosed a sharply graded, but nonetheless well-cared for lawn.

Three black girls in thin cotton dresses with bandannas covering their hair and handkerchiefs over their noses ran barefooted out of the house and down to the gate to meet us. They told us the reason for the handkerchiefs was that the house had been fumigated for termites that morning and hadn't been completely aired out as yet. Frau Kupferman apologized and asked if we would mind waiting for a later lunch. She said that we were welcome to come into the house if we cared to, but perhaps it might be better if, for the time being, we took a walk or relaxed on the lawn chairs.

Sheldon couldn't wait to get to that invitingly cool ocean below, so we left our cases with the girls and followed their instructions, heading toward one of the least hazardous trails down to the shoreline.

Sheldon had taken my hand and we were running across the road and through the tall grasses with their colorful adornment of wildflowers. I found myself sprinting. It seemed effortless and suddenly I felt capable of anything, of leaping and perhaps spinning in the air like a frisky kitten. It had to do with this type of living, I thought. Without even trying, I had lost those five or six excess pounds which had begun to make me both look and feel a bit matronly. For another thing, there was a great release in no longer being concerned with my looks, along with a freeing of the time it consumed to reach cosmetic perfection and, most importantly, a psychological relaxation about my appearance. When you become accustomed to seeing yourself without artificial enhancement, you realize that you no longer judge yourself by some glossy, superficial standard. That had much to do with Sheldon, who claimed that I was beautiful without makeup. He had asked me if I would please, just for him, simply step out of the shower and dry myself without adding paint or curls. When he had seen my natural look, he couldn't stop playing with the ends of my hair or caressing my face with his fingertips. I certainly had no intention of spoiling that flattering attention by returning to an artificiality which displeased him.

Sheldon stopped beside an enormous tree which leaned toward the beach from the very edge of the steep trail. He rested his back on its broad trunk, reclining backward over the precipice and drawing me toward him in a precariously angled embrace. For a split second my breath caught in fright and I hesitated to yield. Then I surrendered my weight, giving my body to him and the tree, even to the boulders below should they wish to take it.

The length of my body stretched along the length of his, my head turned so that our cheeks touched. He had his arms snuggly folded about me. I allowed my arms to drop forward and with them I felt past the firm smoothness of him, to the rough bark of the tree, to my fingers dangling loosely in space.

It was as if we were weightless and drifting gently on flowing currents of sea breeze, as if flying through a celestial bliss on the trunk of that sturdy tree. Sheldon resting on his back facing the sky, I resting on him and the tree, facing the sea. Trusting the sea, the mountain, the boulders, and our tree, and trusting the young man.

He squeezed me and nuzzled his face into my neck. Then he

lifted me up and I returned to earth with my feet planted firmly on the ground.

I looked down at the deep drop and the perpendicular trail which five short days ago might have appeared to me as a treacherous, completely impossible challenge. But on this day it was no longer impossible, only a challenge.

Sheldon stood beside me, his arms around my waist, and seemed to be reading my thoughts: "Don't be afraid, my darling."

I said, "No." I must have said it very solemnly because it made him laugh.

He kept holding me, saying, "Don't be afraid, my darling, it's not so bad as it looks. Concentrate on your footing. One step at a time. Be secure in one position before you reach for the next. You can hold onto certain trees and boulders and when the earth is soft, dig in the heels of your boots. I'll go first and always keep just in front of you. I won't take your hand. That's how most accidents happen. With the best of intentions another person can actually cause you to fall. Rely on yourself. Only you can judge your pace and footing. Do you trust me?"

I said yes without hesitation because it was true; I trusted him implicitly.

Before taking his first step past the tree and down the path he held my chin and kissed me fleetingly on the lips as if to say, "Good, let us go."

Then he startled me by turning and saying over his shoulder, "I love you, you know."

He said it casually, as if he had said it hundreds of times before. He said it simply, as a matter of fact, as if I had known it for a long while. And perhaps I had.

During our descent, he showed no concern about my ability to complete the obstacle course, and his confidence reinforced my own. The challenge was invigorating and soon became of itself the object of the exercise.

Near the end of the trail we had a choice: to the left, a white virgin beach that stretched as far as the eye could see, or to the right, a dainty cove bordered by granite rocks and fringed with red flamboyant trees. Sheldon hesitated and when I was directly behind him, he put his arms straight out from his sides, allowing me to choose the direction. I considered for a moment and then playfully struck down his right arm, indicating the cove.

We were able to slide the last few feet of the path onto the sand of the triangular beach. Once enclosed by the mountain on one side, the granite cliff on the other, and with an expanse of ocean before us, we might have been all alone in the world. Absent were the murmurs of people or engines; we heard only the singing of birds and the hypnotic sound of waves, waves that rolled off an aquamarine sea to caress a powdery white cove, surrounded by a profusion of flaming red blossoms on the aptly named flamboyant trees.

With a burst of impishness, Sheldon threw off his clothes and ran into the ocean. I had only gotten as far as removing my boots when he was frolicking in the surf and presenting me with a full view of his lithe, unbreeched body. I couldn't help being just a bit shocked by Sheldon's total disregard of modesty.

Some agonizing moments went by while I contemplated whether or not to take off any more of my clothing. Sheldon was swimming now and I was glad that he wasn't observing me as I unfastened, then refastened, then again unfastened my trousers before quickly slipping them off. My safari jacket was long and when I stood up it reached to the hem of my panties. But I thought I must surely look silly dressed in a long-sleeved safari jacket but no trousers. So I unbuttoned the jacket, took it off, and put it to one side. There was nothing wrong with being on a beach in bra and panties. It was like being in a two-piece bathing suit. However, Sheldon was already naked and when I thought about it I knew that I wanted him to make love to me. No doubt we were going to make love, so why be so coy about taking off my bra and panties? I wasn't sure I wanted Sheldon to see my nude body in bright sunlight.

I stifled a sudden laugh. For a second I had actually thought about being nude but burying myself in the sand with only my head uncovered.

Sheldon was swimming a long way out. I hurriedly took off my bra and panties and rolled them in my trousers. Then I lay down in the lovely white sand and covered myself by using my safari jacket as a blanket.

The heat of the sand felt sensuous on my skin and that tingling sensation I'd had on and off all day in anticipation of making love returned.

I found myself stretching and yawning and willingly surrendering my naked body to those shifting grains, finally abandoning myself to the sun and my senses to the perfume of the trees and the lullaby of the sounds.

My eyes were closed and I hadn't heard Sheldon approaching, nor had I expected him to return quite so soon. My first awareness of him was when I felt him carefully remove the safari jacket which I had been using as a shield.

Then warm moist lips brushed my cheek and little droplets of bouncing diamonds fell from his eyelids to mine. Having first brushed them across my cheek, the swell of his lips now touched mine. They pressed and parted, and I tasted their saltiness and the luscious sweetness of his tongue.

His hand traced a rivulet of water from my eyebrow down the side of my face, passed the curve of my jawline onto the soft part of my neck and slowly down my chest and the curve of my breast.

The soft heated sand beneath me contrasted with the hard, cold body resting on top of me. For a time he lay perfectly still, the pressure of his body delicate, yet somehow insistent. Demanding that I, too, remain still. I did nothing, yet I felt the heat from me flow into him and warm away the chill of the sea. I didn't move and in the stillness I absorbed something of the essence of him.

Then I was lost. I was lost in responding to his touches as though the caresses of love play were unknown to me and being experienced for the first time.

He made love to me slowly and gently and to the point of madness. He languished over the exploration of my body until I was fully giddy with arousal. He made love to me completely with an awareness and understanding which should have been far beyond his years. This sensitive, gentle boy had the calculated wisdom of a true sensualist.

Neverending moments were suspended and acute, acute and suspended, and our motions were urgent although unhurried and we were sensing our bodies, now individually, now jointly, as we lifted and rose to total fulfillment in an ecstasy of timelessness.

CHAPTER SEVEN

We discovered sometime later that there were no termites on Mahé and that the guest house had been needlessly fumigated. As it turned out, Frau Kupferman was positively haunted by the idea of crawling things and dirt, and could imagine filth even on freshly scoured surfaces. Along with the three black girls who worked for her, she cleaned the house continuously, as though in desperate pursuit of a tranquility born of purity.

Sheldon and I had a cozy, inviting bedroom at Frau Kupferman's. Actually Sheldon had booked two bedrooms, but now that we were lovers we needed only the one. The room we chose had a terrace with a magnificent vista of the Indian Ocean through the spirally grouped leaves of pandanus trees, making it utterly romantic. And while we were like honeymooners, with little will-power to relinquish our amorous embraces or even step foot out of bed, our privacy was perpetually shattered by the frenzied housekeeping activities.

The evening of our first day on Mahé, after we had made love in the cove, we couldn't bear to be out of each other's arms and went to bed immediately after dinner. We had just gotten tucked into the four-poster and begun snuggling when we heard the handle on our bedroom door twisting. I slipped on my robe and upon opening the door discovered one of the girls on her knees polishing the knob. While in a passionate embrace, we heard a carpet sweeper being pushed in the hall and knocking against our door frame. At the very crack of dawn I saw the straws of a broom slipping in and out beneath our door.

Perhaps in her obsession with cleanliness, Frau Kupferman found sex a dirty habit which soiled her premises, leaving the house tarnished in some way. Whenever we returned from even the earliest breakfast, there was never a question of going back to bed or even remaining in our quarters. The terrace was drenched from a recent hosing and the ceramic tiles of the bedroom floor were sticky and smelling of disinfectant. The chintz cushions belonging to the couch were damp and resting on the terrace railing, and our bed had been stripped of everything including its cotton mattress, which stood on some chairs in the corner of the room airing out as if in punishment for its part in the sullying.

However, we didn't trouble her with our unchaste behavior beyond the first days, because we learned how we might go island-hopping and then used our room only as a place to hang our clothes and store our excess luggage. The government's motor schooner, *Lady Esmé,* left Victoria Pier twice a week as a ferry bound to the outlying islands. Praslin was second in size to Mahé and of all the Seychelles, it was the one which held by far the most fascination for tourists. The mysterious Vallée de Mai was to be found there, its primeval coco-de-mers rising like no other palms in straight columns a hundred feet high, and their unique fruit so rare and legendary that at one time it was nearly priceless.

Sheldon's plan was for us to sail on the *Lady Esmé* to Praslin. Once we had disembarked, unlike the rest of the tourists who would be walking the tarmac road to the interior, we planned to take the mountain route which passed alongside the waterfall, then climb down to the Vallée de Mai. After having seen the valley, we would work our way down the other side of the mountain to one of the small settlements and hire a donkey cart to transport us to the fishing village of Cote d'Or on Praslin's north coast. Sheldon had been told by the man in charge of the Victoria Tourist Office that in Cote d'Or we would be able to find room and board at the Fishing Lodge. Also at the Fishing Lodge there would be a private boat for hire to take us on day excursions to any of the other seven islands of that chain. After Praslin, we were most anxious to visit Cousin Island, where the sole inhabitants were unusual birds, many of which were found nowhere else on earth. This would be one of the last opportunities to visit there because Cousin was soon to be declared not only a bird sanctuary but a fully protected zone out of bounds to anyone but scientists.

We had done some extensive shopping in the open markets of Victoria and the day we boarded the *Lady Esmé* for Praslin we were dressed like natives in hand-stitched sarongs. We also had locally woven sandals and the same hats worn by everyone. Sheldon had shopped from among the imported cloth for the most beautiful from which to have our sarongs made. The one he had chosen for himself was a leaf design in cleverly varying shades of green. It had been cut straight to wrap around the waist like a skirt. The one he had pictured me in had a white background with giant hibiscus, and it had been cut on the bias to curve around the body and tie over one shoulder. The hemming on both had been done by hand. Ordinarily I might have felt silly in such an exotic costume as that slinky sarong, but it made little difference then, because all I really cared about was Sheldon's reaction. And when he saw me, he got so excited that he purchased freshly cut hibiscus for my hair and strings of seashells and corals and shark's teeth to adorn my neck. The ornaments, however, had been left behind for the island-hopping, and we thought of only the practical needs, such as a pair of lightweight safari boots as an alternative in rough country to our sandals.

Sheldon had his Katmandu shoulder bag and I had a new hand-crafted basket with a few essentials for our stay. He was rapidly teaching me how to travel unburdened by unnecessary baggage or garments. I did have one garment I knew Sheldon would disapprove of but which I felt I couldn't go without; concealed under my sarong was a bathing suit.

We each had a canteen of drinking water, our important documents, and only a handful of personal items to take on the trip. Sheldon was equipped with both a lighter and matches, detailed maps of the island chain, and a compass. Before leaving the house, I'd had Frau Kupferman make some chicken sandwiches for us and I also had purchased and slipped into my basket some chocolate bars for the first day's climb.

The people on board were as mixed as their languages: English and French, and most common of all, a Creole of French-African-Arab. Many different types of dress were represented, as well as many shades of skin. The thin, hard, black men in waistcloths looked African, but the plump, young, brown girls wearing sarongs looked almost Polynesian. The scene was so varied that Sheldon and I hardly stood out by our difference in appearance.

The *Lady Esmé* had been converted into a sightseeing ferry by the addition of wooden benches. She was a gleaming, white eighty-five footer with a single deck shaded by a wooden canopy. Her high wheelhouse appeared small. Because of the coral reef she couldn't dock at the islands, so both her starboard and port sides were hung with numerous small craft of varying types, and two groups had come on board carrying their canoes.

As soon as we had come up the gangplank, Sheldon made friends with her French captain. The captain was eager for news from home and had asked us to stay with him in the wheelhouse so that he and Sheldon could continue their conversation about the latest news from France. Sheldon, of course, had been born and raised in Paris, but I must admit that for long periods I would forget that French was, in fact, his first language. I could never find fault with his English and it was only when I heard him speaking French that I realized he could be just that touch glibber and communicate with just that fraction more ease.

The trip to Praslin took something in excess of three hours. I watched other islands as the *Lady Esmé* stopped far from the beach and the passengers went ashore by small boat. At Praslin we seemed to have stopped even further from shore and I wondered with some concern if we would be picked up again. I was particularly concerned because as it happened, Sheldon and I were the only tourists going to Praslin that day. However, the captain assured us that we would not be forgotten and that he personally would watch for us on each consecutive trip. When we wished to sail back to Mahé, we were to wait on the nearest rocks at about this hour, either Saturday or Wednesday, and wave some piece of cloth.

There was a young native boy and girl disembarking along with us, and we all took off our sandals and climbed down the rope ladder and into a rowboat. Two crewmen rowed us over a long stretch of reef and carefully around the innumerable coral heads which rose beautifully, if threateningly, to just below the surface.

Once we were past the reef, rather than taking the boat all the way to the beach, they stopped in shallow water perhaps five feet from dry sand. The native children, Sheldon, and I waded ashore in a few inches of warm, foamy surf. Then the children turned and watched the oarsmen rowing back toward the ferry, and Sheldon and I turned and with large motions waved to the captain of the *Lady Esmé,* who was a tiny figure in white on her deck.

The native girl and I had identical baskets; mine was merely much newer. I watched the way she placed it on top of her head and supported it with one hand. I imitated her and found it allowed me better balance and more freedom of movement. The basket also felt lighter when carried that way.

The beach was a narrow strip strewn with massive granite boulders. As we walked inland, the boulders congregated to form mountains of boulders that were surrounded by the tropical foliage. There was a sign for the Vallée de Mai with an arrow indicating the way to the tarmac road.

We could hear the rush of water. Around a few more of the loose boulders we began to feel a mist, and knew we were on the path which led to the waterfall.

Another turn and the mist became a fine rain. Suddenly we were among a different, more extravagant foliage where there were huge ferns and an absolute paradise of orchids. Shy, common orchids on willowy stems peeked from the moss, and bold orchids of yellow and orange and tiger stripes brazenly draped from trees and shrubs. I gasped at the sight. I must have gasped loudly because the children who had been ahead of us came back to see what had happened. I pointed to the masses of orchids hanging in front of me, but these precious flowers were commonplace to the native children and they didn't understand my reaction. They thought I must be pointing to the difficult trek alongside the waterfall. With great pride they showed us that there was a winding tarmac road that one could take instead. Then they proceeded on their way again, not waiting for us to follow.

The waterfall was narrow and angled to the right so that we could not see its height. At times it looked like a winding staircase flowing from above. The large black stones within it were glossy and of intriguing shapes—some were hollowed, others jagged ledges, and still others were flat like the smooth surface of a shower floor. As there were no tourists to avoid, there was no need for us to break a trail up the mountain. It was terraced and not difficult to climb even in bare feet, and staying close to the waterfall seemed irresistible.

The climb made us thirsty and we cupped our hands and drank the wonderful icy water. I knew that Sheldon was going to do it the second before he climbed under the waterfall. It would have been unlike him to miss the opportunity of such an invigorating experience. He put down his sandals and bag and unwound the cloth from his waist revealing those sequestered parts of his anatomy which I found I loved to observe. He edged onto a flat-topped stone and allowed the pure, gushing water to envelop him while he pranced about to take away the sting of the chill.

Shortly we turned and could no longer see the beach. We had wound into a mountain pass. From that point on it was a more difficult climb up to what we had thought was the summit, but we again wound into a mountain pass. When the trail opened, we seemed to have reached a plateau. It was cut deeply by a narrow stream which proved to be the source of the waterfall.

Traveling down from the plateau, we were suddenly overwhelmed by the realization that we were in the Vallée de Mai because we were dwarfed by a prehistoric forest of gigantic trees. They were not ordinary coconut palms. They must have been over a hundred feet high, rising directly to the sky and waving immense palm fronds forty or fifty feet in length.

The sunlight filtering through those densely overlapping fronds was a pale, eerie green, and we were overcome by the feeling that this was not a welcoming place. No animal life seemed to be stirring within the valley. One would have expected thousands of living things in such a dense tropical atmosphere, but it was deserted. The only sounds we heard were the distant rushing of the waterfall and the rustle of palm fronds. We spent our time there without seeing a bird, an insect, or any small mammal and if we had, we might have assumed that they, like us, were merely passing through this forest which seemed to discourage our presence.

The valley was the exclusive dwelling place of the mysterious coco-de-mer *(Ladoicea maldivica),* the only spot in the world where these palms grow. There were male and female trees, and their fruit was an astonishing sight to behold. The female seednut was a double coconut. Observing it from one angle you could see a pair of shapely buttocks, looking remarkably like that of a beautiful woman, and turning it, a tuft of what could have been pubic hair around perfectly etched vaginal lips. The male tree bore heavily scented yellow flowers and its catkin looked for all the world like a green, prickly three-and-a-half-foot-long penis.

There were two stories that explained the name coco-de-mer: one was that the males and females left the trees at night, slid down the waterfall, and made love by the sea. The other was that before the discovery of their secret valley home, it was thought that the trees grew directly up from the bottom of the ocean, and hence the name coco-de-mer.

In early times the seednuts which washed ashore in India and the Maldives were sold for vast prices as they were believed to contain an aphrodisiac. Nothing was known of the male catkin. Having no hard shell, once off the tree they quickly perish.

There is another story that a king in the seventeenth century was turned down when he offered a staggering price of four thousand gold florins for one of the voluptuous female fruits.

Scientists have not proven how pollination is affected from the pendulous male catkin to the giant female fruit, which undoubtedly helps to fuel the legend of their possible nocturnal activities.

Although the seednuts are heavy, some weighing as much as ten or twelve pounds, Sheldon and I each wanted to possess one. As soon as we had collected from the ground the nuts we wanted, we headed with haste out of the valley by following the compass east by northeast.

The Vallée de Mai is without question a mysterious paradise and the experience of being there something to treasure forever, but after we had seen it, we did not wish to linger.

It took us about an hour to work our way down the other side of the mountain to just within reach of a settlement. There we rested in a grove of cinnamon trees and ate our sandwiches.

The houses of the settlement were odd-looking because they were made from slabs of granite, but roofed with thatched palm fronds. It turned out that nearly every family owned a donkey. I felt sorry for any poor beast that would have to pull both Sheldon and me, so we hired two donkey carts for the trip to the north coast. Sheldon paid two Seychelle rupees, or about thirty-five cents, for the transportation and he gave the boy who guided us a rupee as a tip.

Praslin had a wealth of agriculture, and during the long bumpy cart ride we passed more groves of cinnamon, along with banana, pineapple, lime, orange, mango and, of course, coconut. There were also fields of tea plants, potatoes, and melons, as well as bushes hung heavy with pomegranates and pawpaws.

The Fishing Lodge was a long, low structure built the same as the houses: granite with palm-frond roofing. Sheldon had to do all the talking, whether it was to the natives of the settlement or the man and his sons who ran the lodge. Even he had difficulty at times communicating with those who spoke Creole, but at least with his French, everyone seemed to more or less understand what he was trying to say. He was able to arrange a motor boat for the following morning with, for some reason, both the owner's sons as crew. They would take us to Cousin Island.

The lodge accommodations were rather primitive. For all guests, there was one large bedroom with rows of narrow bunks. There was a community bathing room, an indoor and an outdoor w.c., and the dining hall had long tables where everyone sat together for meals. The meal we had that first night would have made a gourmet squeal with delight. The only guests were Sheldon and me and two big game fishermen from Denmark. The Danes' catch that day had included an oceanic bonito, which they contributed to the feast. The owner, in his preparation of the food, was a true Frenchman. He lightly poached the fish, leaving it succulent, and whipped his own homemade hollandaise sauce. He served as a first course the local delicacy of tern eggs with a side dish of cod roe, and with the fish he gave us candied sweet potatoes, pawpaw, and a salad of hearts of palm.

I had never slept in communal sleeping quarters before nor shared a bathroom and I found staying at the lodge a rather daring adventure. I chose to use the outside w.c. because I thought that I should experience everything, if only once. In the morning we took our breakfast of coffee and homebaked bread on the porch where we were visited by brilliant sunbirds, red cardinals, and pure white doves, all eagerly waiting for our crumbs.

Cousin Island was only two miles from Praslin, so we took the opportunity first to circle the waters and have a look at Félicité, Mary Ann, and Les Soeurs. Then on the way to Cousin, Sheldon borrowed a pair of swim trunks that the boys had in the boat and we took another excursion so that he could water-ski. Cousin had a treacherous coral reef, which was why we needed both brothers. It had to be watched for on each side of the boat lest we hit it and scrape a hole in the hull or damage the motor.

The owner of the lodge was Caucasian but he must have been married to an African woman because the sons were mulattos. They were tall and slim, young, and extremely shy. They hardly spoke to Sheldon, and perhaps they hadn't come into much contact with women at the Fishing Lodge because they seemed too timid even to look at me.

We had a perfect day on Cousin Island, swimming, bird-watching, making love, eating our picnic lunch, and napping during the heat of the day under the shade of a palm. At around three o'clock we began looking for the boys and their motorboat, and we noticed that the tide was running out very, very rapidly. There was more and more beach by the minute. When we saw the boys they were a long way out, and calling to us. I don't believe Sheldon was able to distinguish the words, but he had grown progressively quieter as the beach had increased in the receding tide. He had known that the water was too shallow for the boat to come in for us. In my ignorance I suggested that we go slowly and try to swim out to them.

"My darling, the coral reef is exposed," he said, taking me in his arms. "This is obviously some kind of a freak tide. But the boat can't get over the reef and if we tried to swim, it would tear the flesh from us."

There was nothing we could do. We had to wait until morning and hope that the boat would be able to get into shore.

That night, sleeping under the stars was thrilling and hardly a sacrifice. Oh, we were a little hungry in the morning after having gone without an evening meal, but we still had water in our canteens and the situation was not serious. We began to fret when the boat arrived around ten A.M. at what should have been high tide, and the coral reef was still exposed so that the boys had to go away yet again.

By that evening when they came and we couldn't get off the island, we began worrying in earnest. We still had some water, but by then we were very hungry. Except for coconuts that were too high for us to reach, we saw none of the fruit trees that we had seen on Praslin and could see nothing to eat. Finally we found a coconut that had fallen to the ground, but as much as he tried to smash it open between two rocks, Sheldon could not crack the hard shell without the right kind of tool.

The following morning when we still could not get off the island, Sheldon remained calm, but I began to panic. I was famished and there were only a few drops of water left in my canteen. The idea of us dying on the island before we could be rescued seemed a very real possibility.

I went in frantic search of birds' nests. All those thousands of different birds, but where were the nests? Where did they leave their eggs? How I wished that I'd had some knowledge of ornithology. I could find nothing. Sheldon again went to search the interior of the island for food and water.

I sat down with my back against a palm tree and tried to reason how a human being under these circumstances might survive. As I sat there I saw out of the corner of my eye a colorful lizard working his way down the trunk of the tree toward me. He was moving slowly and as I watched him, I began thinking about eating him. He didn't appear merely tolerable in a dire emergency—he looked delicious.

I refrained from killing the lizard, but seeing it had given me the idea of shellfish. Surely the tide would have left behind some mussels or urchins; perhaps I could use my basket as a trap to catch fish. So that is how I spent the long day, dragging my basket in the sand and the water. Still I found nothing. There must have been shellfish trapped on the reef, but they were inaccessible to me.

That afternoon the boat still could not get in for us and a feeling of desperation overtook me. I didn't understand how Sheldon could remain so calm. But he had been fighting illness his entire life and had become a fatalist. He sent chills through me by calmly stating that if he were going to die, he would like it to be in my arms, in such a heavenly place.

Becoming aware of his resignation, I grew more determined to survive. I never truly had been hungry before. Most maddening was my thirst. With manic determination I decided to catch a lizard and suck the fluids from its body. Once I had made my mind up, I began chasing several lizards frantically so that they all scurried out of my reach. Then I willed myself to be calm. Patiently I waited beside an anthill, which was popular with the lizards. I buried my basket partway in the ant-covered sand, and when the next lizard entered, I pounced on the basket, holding it shut. I reached in carefully and after many tries was able to grasp hold of the wiggling creature. If it attempted to bite me, I was not aware of the sting.

I raised the lizard to my mouth, clamped it between my teeth, and shutting my eyes, tore its head off. I spit out the head and with mighty pulls, sucked the fluids from its body. Then I tried to eat the flesh but it was rubbery, and its scales bruised my tongue and the inside of my mouth. But the juices tasted wonderful, like oyster, so I caught another and another and another. Finally I caught one and offered it to Sheldon.

He made a great show of behaving like a savage. He laughed a deep, frightening laugh, tore off the head, sucked the fluid, and chewed and ate the entire thing while making terrible smacking noises.

We were emotional and perhaps even a bit delirious. Something had possessed us and we began laughing as if we'd lost our sanity. We began roaring up and down the beach, chasing lizards, birds, and anything that moved and we did it with great relish as if it were the most exhilarating game either of us ever had played. We kept roaring with laughter as we chased the rare birds. When I screamed out that it was necessary to make this island a sanctuary to protect the birds from cannibals like us, we rolled in the sand in gales of uncontrollable laughter.

We got up and began the chase again: lizards, a solitary mouse, and any birds which landed while we continued to roar up and down the beach with maniacal laughter. Then behind some boulders I saw an awkward, waddling bird. Huge and white, it was an albatross, as surprised to see me as I it. Caught in a confined space between the boulders, it was unable to move out of my path. I threw myself on the albatross and without stopping to consider, I strangled it.

Sheldon made a fire and we roasted it, eating every ounce of flesh and fat and chewing the bones and crying for the sheer joy of no longer suffering the pains of hunger.

Sometime during the night, the range of the tide stabilized. By morning the boys from the lodge were able to come ashore for us. The first thing they did was to offer us water. Sheldon and I gratefully took one long drink each from the canteen. However, Sheldon had brought down to the water's edge that stubbornly sealed coconut which we had found three days earlier and over which we had become so desperately frustrated. We wanted the satisfaction of quenching our thirst with its milk. One of the boys got a machete from the boat and with a quick sharp blow split the coconut open. Sheldon and I eagerly took a half each and raising them, greedily drank every drop of the warm and surprisingly sour coconut milk.

We had made up our minds that we would not allow that terrifying experience of being stranded to interfere with our plans for enjoying the remainder of our stay. Sheldon even water-skied back to the Fishing Lodge.

I had gained an awareness of myself which was disconcerting: there was within me this savage being. I was disturbed by the knowledge not only of its presence but of its ferocity, its capacity to kill, and its ability to do so with such comparative ease. Yet it always must have been lying in wait, otherwise how could it have been unleashed with such swiftness? And now that my actions on Cousin Island had united me with it, I never again could feign innocence of that killer instinct.

ABOVE: The vista through the tall trees of the North Point on Mahé Island was extraordinary. Of all the Seychelles Islands, which number around a hundred, Mahé was one of the four populated when we were there.
BELOW: The east coast of Mahé, looking north to Victoria.

ABOVE: This cove, bordered by granite rocks and red flamboyant trees, is where Sheldon and I first made love.
BELOW: We returned to our cove after an invigorating swim.

ABOVE: The government's motor schooner, *Lady Esmé*, took us to Praslin, the most popular of the Seychelles Islands.

BELOW: I took the lead of a native Seychellois girl and found that this was the easiest way to carry a basket.

ABOVE: The beautiful, yet eerie, Vallée de Mai. Here the coconut palms grow to over a hundred feet tall, and bear the mysterious coco-dé-mer.

BELOW: The waterfall which led us to the Vallée de Mai.

ABOVE: The male catkin of the coco-dé-mer. I need not explain the resemblance, nor why so many legends have sprung up around how pollination is effected between the seednut and the catkin. BELOW: The female seednut, which resembles from one angle shapely buttocks, from another vaginal lips.

From a distance Cousin Island looked inviting, but its dangerous coral reefs made it nearly impossible for us to leave.

ABOVE: Sheldon signalling for the boat that would eventually return us to the main island.

RIGHT: I didn't mind fishing in a more traditional fashion when I wasn't quite as hungry as I was on Cousin Island.

CHAPTER EIGHT

On the plane back to Nairobi, Sheldon and I reminisced about those ten extraordinary days we had spent on the Seychelles, but we were hesitant to remind one another of having been stranded on Cousin Island. We spoke about the botanical gardens of Mahé, of actually having seen flying foxes and gargantuan land tortoises and the world's only black parrots. We discussed in detail everything about the Vallée de Mai; the climb beside the waterfall, the eeriness of the forest; and we freshly examined the seednuts we were bringing back as souvenirs.

We spoke of how I had changed my behavior so much that one day toward the end of our stay, I actually had hit over the head and stunned an enormous crab, then took it to Frau Kupferman asking her to please boil it for our dinner. We laughed when recalling how the poor Frau almost fainted at the sight of the revived crustacean scurrying across her polished kitchen floor. But we carefully avoided mentioning the incident on Cousin Island when I had strangled the albatross.

This time in Nairobi, I willingly checked into the hostel with Sheldon. Thanks to his influence, I was beginning to qualify as a travel bum. At any rate I had begun to develop a passion for that rougher, more spontaneous way of living.

We were in a hurry to shower, unpack, make our phone calls, and get to the veranda of the New Stanley as soon as possible during our first morning back.

When I showered, I looked at myself in the full-length bathroom mirror. What I saw was brown and healthy, slightly muscular,—an amazingly firm-looking body. The image set me to daydreaming. I imagined that the woman who owned that body was not yet approaching middle age. Such a body surely belonged to a younger woman. A strong, capable woman who had the ability to survive under adverse conditions. I didn't know if others would find it beautiful or sensuous, but I was enamored of that body to the point that it made me blush if I dared to think of it as belonging to me.

Sheldon and I had a large, old-fashioned bedroom on the second floor of the hostel. It was at the head of the circular staircase and just across from the hall telephone. It had been after ten that morning when we had checked in and it was nearly eleven by the time I had finished my shower. Both Sheldon and I were anxious to get to the veranda of the New Stanley before the morning was over, but after ten days of being incommunicado, we each had to make telephone calls.

As I came down the hall from the bathroom, I saw that Sheldon was already using the phone. There were no other guests on our floor at that hour so when I entered the bedroom, I left the door ajar. I did it without thinking because I hadn't meant to eavesdrop, but I'm afraid I could hear quite clearly everything Sheldon was saying to his *maman*. I understood enough French to know that he was saying he wanted to stay longer in Africa, he wanted to organize a first-class safari, and he required the transfer of additional funds. I was sorry to be privy to that conversation because his tone with his *maman* was quite different than it was with others. When he met with some resistance about the additional money, the only way I could describe his tone was petulant. He had reverted to the helpless, sickly child who had known no other way to fight for himself. But I didn't care to think of my lover as resorting to petulance on any occasion. At that moment I knew I could never be in the same company with Sheldon and his *maman*. Suddenly, I shuddered. A shattering thought had crossed my mind: his mother might only be five or six years older than me! I quickly shut the door so I could no longer hear Sheldon's conversation and tried to think about something else.

I had promised to call Sally MacKenna as soon as we returned to Kenya to let her know we were back safely. And as I had left her as my contact, I wanted to get from her any news she might have for me from America or Italy. But no sooner were we connected than Mac took the receiver away from Sally to give an urgent message to Sheldon and me. He began speaking rapidly: "Listen, the animals are on the move across the Serengeti! You have a rare opportunity to see the big migration! But you'll have to hurry! It began early this morning and it only lasts a few days. You and Sheldon will have to get to Tanganyika as quickly as possible. I am leaving myself in a few minutes. I was able to contact the Frasers and they are on their way. Fortunately, I've got a friend who is saving space for us at his tented camp. Now take down these instructions. Have you got something to write with?"

I called to Sheldon: "Darling, it's Mac. He says that we have to get to Tanganyika right away if we want to see the animals on the move! Can you come here and bring something to write with?"

Sheldon came flying out of the bedroom in dancing leaps, forgetting to bring a paper and pencil. "The migration across the Serengeti plains?! My God, all the times I've been in Africa. I've always missed it before!"

Mac was saying: "Everybody is heading there without reservations. You could go on your own simply by driving across at the nearest border point, but I'm afraid all the lodges and camps will be full. Ann and Dick Fraser are flying in from Masindi to Arusha and Arusha's a short flight for me from Tsavo. If you want to join us, we are meeting up this afternoon at the Hotel Arusha."

I interrupted him: "Just a second, Mac. Hold on."

I was about to call again to Sheldon to bring me something to write on when he arrived with a notebook and pen. "Okay Mac," I said into the phone. Sheldon was nodding vigorously in approval and holding the notebook flat for me while I wrote: *Hotel Arusha.*

Mac continued, "All right, then you will have to hire a private plane to fly you to Sanya Juu Airport and from there it is a ten-minute taxi ride into Arusha. We won't be staying at the Hotel Arusha, we will just use the veranda as a meeting place. I'll be getting there first, so I'll make sure the jeeps I've reserved are ready for us. We'll be staying at Jove's Tented Camp at Ngorongoro, but we have to pick up the Land Rovers in Arusha."

I asked, "How do you spell that place where we'll be staying at a tented camp?"

"Just write down the big crater," Mac said. Then he added, "Sally wants to talk to you for a second, so I'll pass you to her. But then get going with those arrangements for a private plane. We want to get to Ngorongoro before nightfall."

I was sorry to hear from Sally that she would be unable to join us. During the season, they couldn't both leave the game lodge. Sally gave me the names and phone numbers of two private companies who worked out of Nairobi Airport, and I was able to book with the first one that answered. It was an expensive business hiring a private plane and I wasn't surprised that not everyone could afford the luxury of traveling that way.

Sheldon was still leaping up and down. He stopped only long enough to hug me and then began jumping again. Tugging on his shirttail, which had pulled out of his trousers, I yelled, "Darling, darling! Listen for a moment. Please. Our plane is ready for takeoff in two hours. Do we have time to go to the New Stanley veranda before leaving?"

"Yes, my clever darling," he said hugging me and causing me to jump up and down with him. "Yes, my adorable, newly inaugurated travel bum, let's run to the New Stanley and spread the news about the migration."

We hurriedly repacked our half-unpacked suitcases, stored them downstairs in the hall, and paid the bill. Then we held hands and literally skipped the two blocks to the New Stanley. We were not given the pleasure of making the first announcement about the migration because when we arrived the veranda was buzzing with talk of nothing else. The veranda had become like a large party of friends, table-hopping in an effort to collect all available information and compare notes. We encountered some people who were disappointed that their plans prevented them from getting to the Serengeti, others who were still trying to make up their minds about going, and still others like us who were about to set out on the journey. But there was not a single person on the veranda uninterested in discussing the exciting news that the big migration had begun only hours earlier.

I looked for Bert, Cathy, and Susan in her wheelchair. This was the day of our appointment and I really had been looking forward to seeing them again. I hoped they had heard the news about the Serengeti and would have an opportunity to go there. I reasoned that perhaps that was why they were not keeping the appointment; perhaps they had heard and already had set out in Bert's camper.

Just then a sparkling clean red-and-white camper truck pulled up on the street just below the steps of the veranda, and Susan and Cathy were both waving and calling to me. Taking the steps two at a time, I was leaning in the passenger window and kissing them on the cheek almost before Bert was able to get out of the driver's side and come around to me.

We were all talking at once and saying the exact same things: "Did you hear about the migration?"—"The Serengeti!"—"Are you going?"—"Of course we are!"—"So are we! Isn't it exciting?" —"It's a rare opportunity."—"You have to be on the plains just at the right time."—"They say that people can come to Africa year after year and have the bad luck of missing it."—"Yes, that has happened to Sheldon!"—"It started this morning."—"We'll have to hurry, it only lasts a short time."—"So then you're going?"— "Yes, we are setting out right away."—"Great! So are we!"—"Terrific! Where will you be camping? Can we meet up?"

They thought meeting us at the big crater was a super plan. Going the entire distance by road, it would take them much longer to get to Ngorongoro, but Bert planned to drive nonstop. He believed that by pushing ahead they could reach the campsite by early morning.

In arranging our charter to Arusha, I had requested a two-engine plane and a highly experienced pilot. I hoped to minimize the risks, as getting to Tanzania meant crossing mountains. Flying south toward the border, shortly after having passed over Tsavo, Mount Kilimanjaro stood before us.

At home on my bookshelf was a well-worn copy of Hemingway's *The Snows of Kilimanjaro,* on the cover a photograph of the western summit. Had I been blindfolded, not known which continent it was, I believe I would have recognized her by that familiar snow-capped dome. Here I was actually seeing her, and I was all at once very moved and realized I was crying. I remembered Hemingway's description of how Harry had seen her at the moment he knew he was dying: "There, ahead, all he could see, as wide as all the world, great, high, and unbelievably white in the sun, was the square top of Kilimanjaro. And then he knew that was where he was going."

In 1971 there wasn't an airport in Arusha, but the flat open plains of Sanya Juu made a natural landing field. From the Sanya Juu plains one could observe Kilimanjaro rising from the savannah and dry lakes of the Nyiri Desert.

The entire landscape was born of volcanic eruptions; from the cones of Kilimanjaro and Mount Meru forty-four miles to the west, to the lava-formed lakebeds and volcanic depressions of the crater mountains to the east. There was the charming miniature Ngurdoto crater and the awesomely huge Ngorongoro with its crater-floor area of two hundred square miles, rising eight thousand feet to its rim.

All these products and structures of volcanic eruptions were associated with the fault line of the Great Rift Valley, where to the west stretched the Serengeti. The greatest number of plains animals anywhere on earth was on the Serengeti.

Nearby was the Olduvai Gorge where Dr. L.S.B. Leakey, curator of the Corydon Museum in Nairobi, had made his famous excavations. The Olduvai Gorge had some millions of years before been a deep-water course and looking up from its dry river bed to the three-hundred-foot-high cliffs on either side, Dr. Leakey had been confronted by a wealth of fossils. Among those he had unearthed were some of the oldest human fossils ever found. We were in a region which represented the essence of Africa and perhaps the very cradle of mankind.

It was a fiercely hot world this time of year, crying out for rain . . . a world smothered by great waves of dust. And when our plane landed, it blew those waves to full storm. The dust storm detained us on board the aircraft until visibility returned and the choking clouds had settled enough for us to be able to walk through them.

When we transferred to a taxicab, the terrible heat forced Sheldon and me to keep the windows open and we arrived in Arusha covered from head to foot in layers of grit. We half-heartedly attempted to brush ourselves off before entering the veranda of the Hotel Arusha, but it was a token gesture and futile. Not only our clothes were dust-covered but grit was caked in our hair, eyelashes, and nostrils.

Seeing that neither Mac nor the Frasers were present on the veranda, I said to Sheldon: "Perhaps after we've had something to drink, maybe a lemonade, if we have time we should rent a room so that we can take a shower?"

"That's not a bad idea, my darling," he replied. "We can leave a message with the waiter. You might want to order a lager. I find beer is the best thirst-quencher in the heat and dust."

I couldn't understand why Mac wasn't there. "Mac must have arrived," I said. "He was leaving before us. He did say he was going to take care of the jeeps first thing. Maybe that's where he is. I think he might have meant to hire three—you know, one for each of us . . ."

Sheldon took my hand and interrupted me. "My darling, I'm not permitted to have a driver's license."

"Of course—it hadn't occurred to me. I suppose you would be at risk if you had a seizure at the wheel. I've got a license but I've never driven a jeep. What do you think? Could I do it? Would you like us to have our own transportation?"

"Might be a good idea," Sheldon said. "You should have an international driver's license but sometimes they overlook that. Certainly you can easily learn to handle a four-wheel drive."

We were seated by the railing of the veranda and only inches from the road. It was a road that, although tarmacked, was quite narrow. When Mac suddenly appeared, he roared toward us and his wheels slipped in the loose dirt. As he skidded to a halt, he sprayed a fresh layer of dust over us, our table, and most regrettably, over our frosted mugs of lager. His own reddish-brown hair, eyebrows, and mustache were tinged with the stuff.

Mac joined us for a beer and before we had gotten around to ordering seconds, the Frasers pulled up in a taxi. In the short time since we had seen them, Ann and Dick had become almost unrecognizable. They were burned nearly black by the sun, and both were much thinner. They had suffered a severe dysentery in Uganda and just recently returned to eating solids.

It was decided that we had better get started just as soon as the rental garage delivered the other two jeeps to the front of the hotel. There were not enough normal-sized Land Rovers, so Sheldon and I volunteered to accept the large seven-passenger one, which was the most awkward to keep on the narrow road. Mac drove in the lead, and trying to keep up with him and the Frasers made my initiation into jeep-driving a true test under fire.

Outside Arusha the narrow road stretched endlessly over barren country. We were driving through a bleak, empty savannah seen through a screen of dust. There was not a single vehicle coming from the other direction, and we saw only a few small animals and one lonely Masai. There were no telephone poles or signs, nothing man-made except that straight tarmac road, and we were compelled to follow it without a hint, it seemed, of ever arriving.

The moment the sun began to set, the temperature of the desert fell drastically and both Sheldon and I became aware of the extreme chill. We were afraid to stop and unpack sweaters for fear of losing touch with our caravan. Nothing apparently ever tempted Mac to stop or even slow down, and the Frasers seemed equally hell-bent on getting to Ngorongoro before nightfall.

The sky had darkened only minutes before we knew that we would reach the safety of Jove's Tented Camp. Lanterns and flaming torches hung everywhere so that we were able to see the camp from a long way off. The lanterns glowing through canvas gave Jove's a most warm and inviting appearance. Around the perimeter, however, the flaming torches stood as reminders that we would be protected from wild animals only by the precarious glowing boundary they provided.

The camp consisted of a dozen or so tents. They were erected in a semicircle facing a low permanent building. In front of this main building was a cement patio where the entire population of the camp seemed to be congregated for drinks when we arrived. There must have been twenty-five or thirty guests, and Mac told us that it was most unusual for Jove's to be so crowded.

One unfortunate concession to civilization was the nearby and very noisy generator. It was needed to light the main building and keep the refrigerators running. But it also operated the crude ice-making machine and when we joined the other guests on the patio for drinks, it was a real treat to be surrounded by wilderness and yet have chunks of ice for our gin-and-tonic.

There were separate bathhouses for the men and women, but each was only large enough for one person at a time. Still, there wasn't a long wait to bathe because in this dry season the water was rationed. Each person got one full bucket placed on a low stool, and one full tin container hung overhead. I used the water in the bucket to soap myself all over and I dunked my head into the bucket repeatedly in order to shampoo my hair. Then I pulled the overhead cord and with the drops of water released through the holes in the bottom of the tin container, I rinsed myself. I did it all very quickly as well, because I was shivering quite badly. The temperature inside the bathhouse was fairly comfortable, having been heated by a kerosene stove, but the water had been carried by porters directly in from the well and it was freezing cold.

I realized that my hair was going to present a real problem from this point on in our travels. It was long and too difficult to dry without an electric hair dryer. I didn't want to go to dinner wearing a towel as a turban, or indeed to go to sleep in the chill night air with a still-wet head. The only solution seemed to be to snip most of it off.

Ann Fraser was next in line for the bathhouse and while she waited for the porters to replace the water, I asked her if she had ever given a haircut. Ann said that there had been times when she had been forced to trim not only her own hair but Dick's as well because they had been far removed from barber shops. I asked her to please help me out.

After her shower Ann came to our tent wielding a long pair of negative-cutting scissors. I was too apprehensive to even watch the operation, and as the first locks of blond hair fell on the canvas floor, Sheldon ran out in horror. But when it was over, holding up the mirror of my compact, I could see that Ann had given me a raggedy but rather fetching short, spiky bob, similar to her own. I was even more pleased when, after a good towel rub, my hair was dry and I began to feel warm again.

Jove Corkingdale was a broad, hard-muscled man who in many ways reminded me of Mac. He, too, was both loud and good-natured, and like Mac, a white man completely devoted to the African way of life. They even looked alike, except that Corkingdale's beard, mustache and hair had turned white. He had been christened Jeremiah Corkingdale but enjoyed telling people that he was really a pagan at heart, so had changed his name to Jove. He didn't even seem to mind the inevitable "By Jove" jokes.

That night Jove took charge of a barbecue. An antelope was roasted whole over an open-pit fire. The spit was a thick iron bar which had to be turned continuously by two African men while Jove, using a long-handled paint brush, kept basting the roasting animal with a spicy barbecue sauce. When the roast was brown and crispy, we all lined up with our tin plates. With grand flourishes of the knife, Jove carved the barbecued meat. The roasted antelope, along with a slab of cornbread for the drippings and a mug of ale, made a delicious meal. Possibly it tasted even better because we were seated on mats around a roaring campfire.

Only once had I slept in a tent and that was at Girl Scout camp many years before. It is a very special feeling sleeping under canvas, and one that I had recalled vividly. Now it was even more of a thrill. I was in East Africa rather than the mountains of Pennsylvania, and when I reached over to the camp bed across from mine, rather than a Girl Scout, I touched my beloved Sheldon.

CHAPTER NINE

They awakened us at three-thirty in the morning by clanging a general alarm on a large tin basin. A second later the flap of the tent was unzipped and thrown back, and a servant entered carrying a lighted kerosene lantern to replace our extinguished one. It was not only pitch black at that hour but the cold was even more penetrating than it had been the night before. Sheldon and I dressed quickly and ran to join the others already gathering around a newly blazing campfire. None of the guests seemed to be grumbling at the earliness of the call. Presumably everyone was there for the same reason. We all hoped and perhaps even prayed that the migration was not yet over and that we might have the opportunity of seeing it, most dramatically by the first light of dawn.

Mugs of strong tea were being passed around, and over the fire in the barbecue pit the waiters had set slices of cheese-covered bread to toast on a long basket rack. There was a buffet table where you got your utensils and napkins, the milk and sugar for your tea, and the mustard and pickles for your toasted cheese sandwiches. It was a most unusual breakfast but it tasted wonderful at such a cold and early hour.

At that time of the morning, one might have expected a more subdued group, but there was a loud commotion from some of those attempting to get dressed (apparently unable to find their footwear) and shrieks from others on entering the outhouses (apparently upon meeting some unexpected occupants.) One felt the flurry of activity and excitement and the chaos caused by those sharp reminders that we were in Africa. While they had been asleep, the residents of certain tents had had their shoes or boots snatched and eaten by hyenas, and the first people into the outhouses were confronted by beetles the size of baseballs.

Jove himself was making a racket by banging with a spoon on a tin basin, asking for our attention. He had appeared all at once between the cooking and campfires, his white hair, mustache and beard gleaming in the reflections from the flames to either side of him. With his arms raised, holding aloft the tin basin, he could have been an ancient god suddenly come amongst us to decree our fate.

"Everyone! Can I have your attention!" he said in a booming voice. "The sky will start to get light in a half an hour. If any of you are ready to leave now, follow me. I don't want you driving the wrong direction and over the rim of the crater!"

Then Jove motioned for Mac to join him and held up Mac's arm to identify him to the guests. "My friend Mac MacKenna here has offered to help as guide. Those of you who want to follow him, be ready at the entrance in exactly twenty minutes. If you're late, you're on your own. Most people are anxious to see the migration at first light."

CARROLL BAKER

He continued to give instructions but my attention was drawn by a tugging at my cardigan sleeve. I turned to see Susan in her wheelchair. I said hello and asked her where Cathy and Bert were, then realized that I was talking too loud and leaned over close to her.

She whispered, "They're both asleep. I slept a few hours last night but Bert drove nonstop and Cathy stayed awake to keep him company."

"Are you settled in here?" I asked.

"Yeah, we made arrangements with Jove to hook up to the generator and use the camp facilities. Then Bert and Cathy went back to the camper and passed out. That was about an hour ago." Then she pulled me a little closer and whispered, "I have to use the toilet. Can you help me?"

"Sure," I said. "Just let me tell Sheldon and get the flashlight from him."

Sheldon mouthed "hello" to Susan. I moved over toward him and told him where we were going. He handed me the flashlight and urged me to hurry, saying we should get started as quickly as possible. He said he would get our Land Rover, pick up Cathy and Bert, and then bring it around to the outhouses for Susan and me.

"What do you mean, darling?" I asked him because I was confused about his driving the jeep.

He pulled me closer and I thought it was to whisper in my ear but instead he took the opportunity to nibble on my earlobe. "I don't have a driver's license, but that doesn't mean that I don't drive," he whispered between nibbles. "Now get going. We want to be in position before the sun comes up."

When Susan and I got to the outhouses and found an unoccupied toilet, helping her from the wheelchair onto the toilet seat proved to be quite a feat on my part. Susan had developed powerful arms and basically she only needed me to hold onto, but without the flashlight we would have been in total darkness. So while she pressed on my shoulders, I not only gripped her around the waist, but I held the flashlight under my chin.

"I'll be okay now, thanks," she said. "I've got some matches here in the side pocket of my wheelchair. You go ahead and I'll call for you when I'm ready to leave."

I barely had time to enter a toilet cabinet of my own before Sheldon had arrived with the Land Rover and began honking the horn. Bert was calling out for us all to "get going," and I heard Cathy in the toilet next to mine helping Susan. In the rush and confusion, I lost my inspiration. My early toilet training had not included performing under duress. That was something I would have to learn to cope with while camping out.

Even though we made every effort to get to the meeting place on time, we missed joining Mac's group. When we reached the exit there was no one else about and the eastern sky already was beginning to show faint light. We felt desperate over being late and Sheldon sped across the savannah trying to make up lost time. However, we had only traveled a few minutes before coming upon the eight or nine jeeps in Mac's group. They were stationary, forming a horizontal line of vehicles. The occupants of the jeeps were all staring intently at the horizon. We spotted Mac, and Sheldon pulled us in beside him and turned off the ignition. Then we became aware of a complete silence. No one was moving about or speaking, yet the atmosphere was highly charged with a mute anticipation.

Rays of vivid lights shot up in advance of the ball of the sun, and a distant roaring accompanied them. At first it seemed to be the light rays themselves exploding with noise. On the horizon a cloud of dust formed and rose with the next brighter sun beams. Within seconds the sky turned a bright white, the dust was rendered transparent, and on the horizon a line of black dots appeared.

The roaring sound grew louder. Then, silhouetted against the fireball of the sun, over the crest of the earth came the herds. The Serengeti resounded to the hooves of the most prodigious congregation of animals to be found on any plain on earth. And they came and came, and they continued to come in thick mounting columns. Thousands upon thousands of animals came pouring across the plains from east to west.

At that distance, as they crossed in front of us, there was an alternating psychedelic effect: at one moment millions of zebra stripes gyrating through a haze of bluish heat waves, at other moments the gray humps and beards of wildebeests streaking past, highlighted by the orange-red light of the African morning; then suddenly only shapes of animals on thundering hooves practically hidden by clouds of dust. All combined to form a dense and steady mass that looked like an endless black locomotive flashing by. On and on and on they came, in their mad rush toward the permanent waters of the western lakes.

We watched spellbound, not quite believing this phenomenon was happening or even possible, for it seemed that they would never stop coming. Earlier, I had meant to ask Mac why he wished to see the migration yet another time. Now I knew. One felt humbled and privileged and a part of the great mystery of the universe. One did not have to be too fanciful to imagine that this day had broken like the first day of Creation.

Within an hour, although the herds were still on the move, we nevertheless went back to camp. It was turning warm and we wanted to shed our sweaters and refresh ourselves. When we started out again, Mac was no longer required to be a guide for the large body of tourists. It was light and they could find their own way to and from the camp, so we alone followed Mac. I drove with Sheldon sitting beside me in the front. Cathy and Bert were on the back stationary seat, and with the extra jumpseats folded up, we had been able to lift Susan straight into the middle portion still seated in her wheelchair.

This time we drove closer to the herds, and watched them from beneath the shade of a flat-topped umbrella tree. Our jeeps were side by side and Mac told us, "Never pull in under a tree unless you've carefully examined the overhead branches. If you don't have a trained eye, it's better to look through your binoculars."

"For snakes?" Cathy squealed. She was looking at the open space between the tree and our topless jeep, and tossing her blond head in alarm.

"No. No tree snakes. Not in this part of the country." Mac laughed. "But look out for the dangling tail of a leopard. Leopards are damned hard to spot when camouflaged in an acacia."

"Ahhh, look!" Susan said holding up our only pair of binoculars for the next person to take his or her turn. "Just look at all the babies!"

Mac, who had his own binoculars, continued to study the herds through them. "Yes," he said, "they're calving early this year. Some of those young gazelles are only hours old. But they'll trot beside their mothers all day long."

Bert, who gallantly refused to have his turn using the binoculars in case he deprived one of us ladies of their use, was studying the herds' movements from the point of view of his army background. "Watch how they wheel together to the left or right, just like a squadron," he drawled. "There never seems to be a command . . . but just watch how they keep closing rank. And those isolated ones are probably sentinels."

"That's correct," Mac said. "They are sentinels, because you'll notice that unlike the rest, they never graze as they go along."

"I see them!" Cathy said. "They're the ones that keep looking out in all directions across the plain."

"What are they on the lookout for?" Susan asked Mac.

"Mainly lions," he replied, "but there will be leopards and cheetahs hiding in some of these trees."

"This entire scene is a photographers' paradise." I said, wishing

I had remembered my camera and vowing to buy myself a new one at the very next opportunity. "I wonder where Ann and Dick are? They must be going mad with joy at the pictures they're getting."

"There will be hundreds of lions following the herds, won't there, Mac?" Sheldon asked him.

"You bet!"

"Oh, I'm longing to see some newborn cubs," Susan cooed.

Mac, who was enjoying the company of the young girls, laughed again. "I'm sure you'll get your chance," he said. "We'll go down into the crater this afternoon."

"But won't all the lions be following the herds?" Susan asked him.

"No, some lions are not migratory," Mac said. "And you'll see all thirty-five species of plains animal in the crater . . . just as if this big migration weren't happening up here on the plain. There will also be a wealth of bird life."

The mention of bird life sent a strange chill through me. Sheldon was so attuned to me that, through his special empathy, he seemed to react to even my innermost thoughts. The moment that strange chill disturbed me, Sheldon took my hands in his and gently squeezed them. Then he turned them over and kissed the palms of those hands that had strangled an albatross.

By ten o'clock the plains were lashed by the fierceness of the sun at that hair's breadth from the equator, and everything was stunned into somnambulism. Then shortly before the sun was due to be directly overhead, no more specks come over the horizon, and the herds that were present scattered into the shade of the bush. At the same time that the herds succumbed to the heat, we ourselves felt we could no longer tolerate the inferno of the open country. According to Mac, even the carnivores halted in their pursuit and an automatic truce prevailed for the duration of that worst heat of the day.

I believe that almost more than a rest everyone would have

wished for a proper wash, but we were allowed just the one shower a day and it had to be saved for the evening when the need for it was felt most strongly. Each tent had had its basin refilled, but washing only your face and hands hardly seemed sufficient after those long hours on the hot, dusty plains. Susan had a supply of rubbing alcohol which she used daily to swab her numb legs in order to keep the skin free from infection. She very generously (if not foolishly in this country, where supplies were hard to come by) had made a present to each of us of a small amount of this cool cleansing agent.

Sheldon and I gratefully took our bottle. We went to our tent where we sealed ourselves in, stripped, and then carefully and sparingly sponged ourselves clean. We even had some rubbing alcohol left. Rather than wisely conserving it for the following day, we put down a blanket and bedsheet, stretched out on the tent floor, and took turns massaging one another. The stimulation proved to be too titillating and developed into a sexual arousal. In the heat of the enclosed tent at midday, our intense lovemaking left us and our bed clothing soaking wet. Now we had nothing with which to wash ourselves except that one small basin of water. As we attempted to wash again, we giggled at the folly of allowing ourselves to become not only drenched with perspiration but sticky as well. Still damp and sweaty, we curled up together. With a feeling of exhaustion accompanied by contentment, we drifted into a deep slumber.

It was Cathy who awakened us that afternoon, coming to the tent to invite us for tea at Bert's camper. It was three o'clock then and much cooler, but we had a struggle waking from our sound sleep. Only the strongest effort of will power got us off the floor, dressed, and out into the camp grounds.

Bert must have sacrificed his nap in order to polish his camper because when we arrived, the outside of it had a newly applied gloss. The inside as well looked sparkling clean. Bert seemed barely able to contain his joy at having us visit and admire his mobile home. It was the first beautiful thing he had ever owned and he had purchased it with his veteran's pension after having been wounded in Vietnam.

The design of the camper truck did appear to be quite ingenious. In a relatively small area, all the necessary furnishings and appliances had been provided, only compact and in miniature. Yet guests could be entertained, because that need, too, had been foreseen. The rear section by the picture windows was devoted to a large square table, surrounded on three sides by red leather pullman couches, and there was space to seat six, eight, perhaps even ten people.

I decided to slide all the way around to the back of the pullman couch. Before I could get in, I had to laugh to myself at the charming way Bert used his handkerchief to shine yet again the already gleaming leather. Sheldon winked at me in appreciation of Bert's gesture and then slid around beside me. Mac made a point of sitting on the side couch next to the beautiful blond Cathy, and Ann and Dick Fraser, each with a lighted cigarette, sat on the other side by the one available ashtray. Bert sat carefully on a small folding chair and surprisingly, it was Susan who served us. To carry the tea and sandwiches, she balanced a tray over the arms of her wheelchair, which left her hands free for serving or wheeling herself back and forth to the kitchen area.

Mac was a broad man and Ann and Dick Fraser, who were about the same height, were quite tall. Nonetheless, we all seemed to fit comfortably into the camper. Only Bert, whether sitting or standing, looked out of place, for he appeared as a giant might maneuvering within a doll's house. And he was the only one not enjoying the tea and sandwiches because he looked as nervous as if he were host to a party of royalty.

Ann and Dick were doing most of the talking. This trip looked as though it was going to be their most successful so far. They were on a high, both talking at once. "The pictures of the migration are an absolute bonus," Dick was saying. "They're something we never expected to get."

"Oh, yes," Ann chimed in, "and we have you to thank, Mac."

"That's right," Dick said. "We'll be eternally grateful that you went to the trouble of contacting us."

"My pleasure," Mac said. "But if you make the cover of *Life* magazine . . ."

"You'll get a credit line," Ann laughed.

"How did you manage to photograph the whole panorama of the migration along the horizon?" Cathy wanted to know.

Ann and Dick said in unison: "With a 180-degree lens . . ."

Sheldon asked, "What other pictures are you interested in?"

"Some more big cats," Dick said. "A leopard springing . . . lion cubs always make saleable pictures . . . and of course, if we could capture the moment of the kill . . . !"

Ann cut in with: "Oh, God, that would really be fantastic. But I guess we're being greedy . . . asking too much . . . the migration is enough of a bonus for one trip."

"Well, you never know," Mac said. "You might just see a kill this afternoon in Ngorongoro."

"Yes, that's one of the fascinating aspects about Africa," Sheldon said in his charming, cultured English. "Sometimes you can go for long stretches without seeing anything of note and then all of a sudden within a few hours, everything happens."

"How exciting!" Susan said. She wheeled her chair around to face Mac. "What will we look for first?"

Mac laughed. "First we've got to get down the side of the crater."

We set out in three Land Rovers. Mac had his, the Frasers theirs, and because Sheldon and I had the large seven-seater, we again took Bert, Cathy, and Susan. Both Sheldon and Bert wanted to drive, but Cathy and Susan screamed for me to take the wheel. I don't think they had that much confidence in my ability, but I believe they thought that a woman would be more cautious driving down the steep crater wall. For safety, only four-wheel drives were permitted, but not long ago, before some tourist paths were created, it had been necessary to put chains on the tires.

Once at the crater, all three jeeps stopped for a few minutes at the rim to look at the view from above. It was a perfectly clear afternoon, and we could see the crater and its circumference boldly outlined. Amazingly, Ngorongoro had a completely unbroken rim; indeed, we were staring at the largest intact crater mountain in the world. From the top, however, the grassy floor looked the size of a football stadium and it was difficult to imagine that it was, in fact, two hundred square miles. Nor did one get the impression that the slopes went down to a depth of two thousand feet.

The path we took was not direct and yet still very, very steep. I think we all felt a relief when we were driving through the wooded areas where we had trees to break the fall of any skidding vehicles. Most of the drive was slow and tortuous. Mac led us with a care to which we were not accustomed from him.

Then all at once, on coming out of another wooded area, we were down onto the grassy floor of the crater. Thousands of animals seemed to be calmly grazing here, apparently unaware of their brethren on the plains above, who were racing madly toward the western lakes. Here at the bottom of Ngorongoro, the conditions were in total contrast to the dry scrub and water-starved plains of the Serengeti. Here there was an abundance of moist grass and plentiful water in the watering holes.

It was an astonishingly quiet and peaceful scene. As a rule nothing very dramatic occurs when you come upon animals. The sentinels look up sharply for a moment and then go back to grazing. A giraffe was surveying us over the top of a distant acacia tree and we were enchanted to see close by some impala looking very much like Walt Disney's Bambi, and those tiniest of antelope, the dik-dik, which stand only a little over a foot high.

There were beautiful, exotic wildflowers and Cathy begged Mac to permit us to walk around. Mac always had his rifle and so he agreed that we could move about so long as we stayed within twenty-five or thirty feet of the jeeps. We lifted Susan out onto the grass in her wheelchair and then, under the watchful eye of Mac with his rifle over his shoulder, we romped and played like children on an outing.

The Frasers were doing some limbering exercises to ease their sore muscles after so many hours of continuous picture-taking. Sheldon and Bert had climbed a tree just for the sport, and Cathy and I were picking wildflowers. Susan, who had wheeled herself near us, was now stationary and watching through the binoculars a weaver bird building a nest of twigs at the very tip of a branch.

Cathy held up an unusual specimen of wildflower for me to see, and as she did so, she glanced in Susan's direction. Then I saw all the blood drain from Cathy's face. She dropped the flower and grasped me by the arm. She seemed unable to speak as she pointed from her kneeling position to Susan's legs.

I looked to where Cathy was pointing and at first I didn't believe my own eyes: Susan's legs had turned almost completely black. Susan was studying the weaver bird through the binoculars and seemed totally unaware that something was happening to her legs. Then Cathy and I both focused in on what the blackness was, and we both screamed at the same time.

Mac swung the gun in our direction, and seeing nothing, looked puzzled.

It was Ann Fraser who recognized what was happening. "Oh, my God," she cried, "Susan is covered in ants!"

"Holy Mother of God," Mac exploded. "Those ants are Siafu! They're man-eaters!"

CHAPTER TEN

"**M**an-eating ants!" Dick was shouting as he ran toward Susan. "Christ, Mac tell us what to do!"

"First pull her away from their line of march," Mac told him. Then tersely, instructing the rest of us: "Get the cans of gasoline. Pour it over her upper body . . . stop them climbing. Susan, get your clothes off!"

Until that moment, Susan hadn't reacted. She had no feeling whatsoever in her lower body and she had watched the ants on her legs with an almost detached horror. Now she was affected by Mac's urgency and our panic, and she virtually ripped away her blouse and the band of her skirt.

Cathy rushed in, and while Susan pushed herself off the seat by pressing her hands on the arms of the wheelchair, Cathy snatched the skirt out from under her. In so doing a few of the Siafu flipped onto Cathy's face. Cathy's screams were piercing, as the ants bore instantly into the soft flesh of her cheek and neck.

Bert, who had begun pouring gasoline over Susan's back, quickly emptied the can, threw it on the ground, and ran to Cathy. She was frantically swatting at the ants on her face, and Bert raised his enormous hand to help her swat them. Then he stopped in mid-swing, realizing that he might hurt Cathy. Hitting them was not the solution, but he was at a loss and stood griefstricken like some helpless Goliath.

Seeing Bert's dilemma, Sheldon shoved our gasoline can in my direction. "Pour some into my hands," he said. I did so and he ran to Cathy's aid.

"Take her hands down!" he ordered Bert. "Take away her hands!"

With the greatest reluctance, Bert forced Cathy's hands from her face. It was essential because she had begun hysterically clawing at her cheek. Then, once her face was uncovered, Sheldon rubbed the gasoline from his hands into the area where they were entrenched.

"It slows them down but it doesn't kill them," he told Bert. "Now I've got to pluck them out. Hold her still."

But there was no need. Cathy was no longer struggling. She was in a half-faint in Bert's arms.

Ann poured gasoline on Susan's chest while I poured some over each of her shoulders. Her body was then sufficiently drenched to halt the upward procession of ants. However, some already had reached the soft part of her belly where they had swiftly lodged themselves, and dozens of others were clinging in the creases beneath her breasts. Susan was feeling the pain now as well as the terror. She was clenching her teeth and moaning in a steady, monotonous hum.

"Let's get Susan into the shade and lay her down on a blanket,"

Mac said. "Sheldon is right. The only thing to do now is to pluck them out one by one."

"I've got a sewing kit with some needles," Ann said searching through her shoulder bag.

Sheldon approached Mac and told him quietly: "I've got all the ants out of her cheek and neck, but I think Cathy has gone into shock."

Looking over at the pale, motionless Cathy, Mac called to Bert: "Get Cathy into the shade and give her a swig of whiskey. There's a flask in my glove compartment." Noticing that Bert was also badly shaken, Mac added, "And have a drop yourself, mate."

Ann and I spread a lap rug underneath a tree while Dick and Sheldon carried Susan over and put her down on it. Then we began the gruesome operation of plucking, tearing, and digging the still-burrowing Siafu out from her torn and bleeding flesh. We were bitten many times ourselves by strays and ants we had failed to crush, or sometimes even in the very process of crushing them.

Because Susan hadn't felt them on her legs, the ants had gotten a head start and the infestation was massive. Some had burrowed so deeply that by the time we had dug them out her legs looked like raw meat. We had no bandaging, no antiseptic. As for the small amount of whiskey remaining in the flask, Mac felt it would do more good for Susan to drink it.

Almost from the first moment the blood began trickling down her legs, the flies had begun buzzing around. We couldn't manage to shoo them away and also concentrate on digging out the ants. And once the gasoline fumes disappeared, the flies came in swarms. Bert, who had left Cathy lying in the shade on the front seat of the jeep, took off his shirt and began briskly fanning the area around Susan in order to discourage them. But it was impossible to keep all the flies off and there was a very real danger of infection.

Throughout the entire nightmarish incident, Mac had seemed levelheaded and in complete control. But when two jackals crept in close to Susan's prone body, as if she already were carrion, Mac frenziedly raised his rifle and poured bullets into them. They flipped into the air and rolled over and over on the ground like stuffed toys.

For the trip back up to the camp, it was too risky for Sheldon to drive the slope and I wasn't feeling anywhere near steady enough, so Bert drove.

We were silent for most of the climb. Then Bert muttered under his breath, "I've got to get my girls to a hospital. Right away. Cathy, too—I don't want her beautiful face scarred."

Cathy was in the back on a jump seat beside the stretched-out Susan, holding her hand. Cathy seemed to be out of shock now, but we were keeping a close watch on her. She had a scarf partially covering the wounded side of her face but the part of her cheek which protruded from the edge of the scarf was badly swollen and discolored.

Bert spoke again, this time turning toward Sheldon and I, who were seated in the front beside him. "We haven't got more than a few hundred dollars," he said softly. "And that's between the three of us. So I've decided to sell the camper."

Sheldon and I looked at one another. We would never allow Bert to sell his camper, not when between us we had more than enough money for hospital treatment. It occurred to me and probably to Sheldon as well that the difficulty would be in getting Bert and the girls to accept money from us.

By the time we reached camp, both Cathy and Susan were shivering in the early evening air, and Susan was burning up with fever. Fortunately, Jove had all the equipment worthy of a small clinic, including a refrigerator section with everything from snake-bite serum to penicillin. We were able to disinfect and bandage the girls and give them each a large injection of penicillin. In the meantime, Mac had gotten on the radio and ordered a plane to meet us by first light at Sanya Juu.

Mac, Sheldon, and I led in Mac's jeep, and Bert followed with the camper in which both girls were resting. We drove to Arusha as fast as we could go at night over the dark road.

Because of the mountains the plane wouldn't be able to come in until it was light. Both girls were sleeping, if fretfully, and we decided that it would be wiser not to move them for those few hours until dawn. During what remained of the night, I sat up to watch over them, allowing Bert to get some sleep. He soon would have ahead of him the long drive into Nairobi. Mac and Sheldon checked into the hotel for a few hours of rest. Sheldon was due to take over from me at four A.M. so that I could go to the hotel and have a shower.

Mac had made arrangements with the hospital in Nairobi, as well as with the chief surgeon who was a friend of his to take charge of Cathy and Susan. Mac, who would nonetheless have headed back to Tsavo shortly, had volunteered to fly with the girls and check them into the hospital. Bert would set out as soon as they were airborne, and Mac would wait at the hospital until Bert got there.

Sheldon and I were determined to take care of all costs, and that was understood with Mac. The bill for treatment would be sent to Mac at Tsavo and then Sheldon and I were going to share the expense. When Sheldon arrived in the morning to take over for me, it would be up to him to tell Bert of our intentions. He would have to convince Bert that it was no hardship for us and that we sincerely wanted to be of help in that way.

Once the plane and camper departed for Nairobi, Sheldon and I were heading back to Jove's camp to spend one more day there with the Frasers. Ann and Dick had only two days left before they were scheduled to fly home to Vancouver. It seemed to me that things happened too swiftly, and it was difficult to know which way to turn. We wanted to be with Ann and Dick on their last day, and yet we wondered if we shouldn't be at the hospital with the girls and Bert.

Sheldon convinced me that since we had planned to be back in Nairobi in a week's time anyway, and Cathy and Susan would need at least that week of hospital supervision, we should continue with our travel plans. Mac would be there today, and the Frasers would be in Nairobi on the following day and visit the hospital.

It was just after midnight, and I mused that this was to be the seventeenth day in Africa for Sheldon and me. We ourselves had only two weeks of the trip left. Sheldon was taking it for granted that we would extend our stay, but I was being a total coward, refusing to think about the future. Each day had been so full that it had been difficult to live beyond the moment. At present I was unprepared to think about a return to civilization, where Sheldon would be considered a misfit . . . and where I knew our paths would have to separate.

I was grateful at that moment for Bert's sudden snore, which roused me from my unpleasant pondering. The front seat consisted of one unbroken cushion, and in his exhaustion, Bert had managed to curl up with his knees resting on the steering wheel.

I got up from my folding chair and went to attend to the girls who were on either side of the double bed, a bed which converted from the large square table and pullman couches. Cathy's temperature was only a few degrees above normal and she no longer looked pallid. I managed to get her to sit up long enough to drink a glass of water and take some aspirin. Susan, on the other hand, seemed delirious and when I took her temperature, I became alarmed. It had risen since the last reading, which had been only half an hour before.

Jove had given me two vials of penicillin. I decided to use them both for Susan. I gave her an injection, with the intention of giving her a second one just before Sheldon arrived at four. Raising her head so that she could swallow, I used an eyedropper to put some water on her tongue. She was burning hot and completely dry, unlike Cathy, who was perspiring normally. Then I remembered how one helped to bring down a baby's fever; I opened her nightgown down the front, quickly rubbing her with a large splash of rubbing alcohol.

I sat down again and in a half daze began to dream of Hemingway's story, *The Snows of Kilimanjaro*. Here on the Sanya Juu plains we were beneath the mountain, in her moonlight shadow. I recalled how in the story, Harry had scratched his right leg and neglected to put iodine on it immediately. Then their truck had broken down, the antiseptic had run out, and the leg had become gangrenous. While the vultures circled ominously overhead, Harry, too, was waiting for a plane to take him to the hospital.

I shuddered, stood up and went to the window. Even fully awake, the events of that day replayed in my head over and over again. The night noises of Africa seemed louder than ever. I could see nothing clearly from the small window, but there were creeping shadows everywhere. I imagined the shadows were those jackals Mac had shot, returning to life and prowling outside the camper, waiting for me to open the door a crack so that they could spring past me and devour Susan.

I checked again that the door was securely locked, then I went over to Susan and gave her a few more drops of water and bathed her lips and forehead. She was so hot that the water evaporated instantly. I leaned down and found myself sniffing the bandages on her legs, trying to discern if there was a rotting smell—the beginnings of gangrene. There was no bad odor. And I told myself that there would be none, not now, not when we had penicillin.

In reality, I had sole responsibility for the girls for only a brief time, but it passed with agonizing slowness and the night seemed to be endless. Just before Sheldon arrived to relieve me, I again bathed Susan in alcohol, gave her water, and injected her with the last of the penicillin. At a few minutes before four when I took her temperature it had begun to fall.

Nevertheless, an hour later as I watched the plane take off and fly over the western summit of Kilimanjaro, I prayed that Susan, unlike the Harry of Hemingway's story, would live to appreciate that sight on many another day.

Sheldon had insisted that I stretch out on the back seat of the Land Rover while he drove us back to Ngorongoro. I was grateful for a chance to sleep and willing to take the risk of him being alone at the wheel. I must have slept very soundly, because I remembered nothing until I'd been gently shaken. We had pulled into Jove's Camp. It had still been early enough for us to have some breakfast. Many people already had set out for the day, but Ann and Dick were anxiously waiting for our report on Cathy and Susan.

We brought the Frasers up to date while we had our coffee and scrambled eggs. Jove stopped by the table to inquire after the girls. When he saw our breakfast, he asked us how we were enjoying the ostrich eggs. As they tasted to me like hen's eggs, I had no idea if he was joking or if they really were ostrich.

Jove told us that the herds were still on the move, but that they had thinned out considerably. This was the third and final day of the migration. We had been very fortunate to see the migration on the second morning when it had still been in full force. Even the weather had been ideal. Today there were thick rainclouds hanging about.

Sheldon was terribly concerned that the rainy season might be upon us unseasonably early. It normally came at the end of March and this was still February, but the rains had been known to come early in some years. And when the rainy season began, its downpours and flooding made travel virtually impossible.

"I've heard that the Siafu leave the anthill just prior to rain," Sheldon said.

"It may rain briefly," Jove told us with utter certainty. "But this is not the beginning of the rainy season."

In reply to our questions as to how he was so sure, he said: "The Siafu ants start on a line of march shortly before a rain . . . on the other hand if it were the big rains, the herds would have migrated last month." He added wryly, "Besides, it can't rain. The lightning birds that are said to be the rainmakers haven't as yet finished building their nests."

"Are those the hammerhead storks?" Dick asked.

"Yes."

"We wanted to get some photographs of them in their enormous platform homes," Ann said.

"You're too early," Jove said. "But if you ever do photograph a rainbird's nest, check it out very carefully first . . . you might find that the occupant is a twelve- to fourteen-foot python. They curl up inside and wait for the birds."

Ann and Dick wanted to get started with the day's work. Tomorrow they were leaving for Nairobi, and the next day for Canada. Although Sheldon and I still felt tired, we didn't want to waste the morning sleeping. The four of us again set off for the crater of Ngorongoro, with me driving our jeep and Ann driving theirs.

When we reached the rim, the heavy rain clouds marred any view of the crater floor. Before descending, I felt a pang of disquiet at returning to the scene of yesterday's horror. Also, I wondered if a sudden downpour came, would that mean we would be trapped at the bottom and prevented from getting back before nightfall to the safety of the camp? But I reasoned philosophically: we called ourselves adventurers, so we had to be willing to take our chances.

CHAPTER ELEVEN

As we worked our way through the last of the forest and emerged onto the crater floor, the clouds lifted and the sunshine poured into Ngorongoro. My attention became focused on a herd of eland grazing directly ahead of us. They appeared to be a huge herd. Eland are the largest antelopes, and the silkiness of their bluish-gray hides was remarkably shiny in the sudden brightness of the cloud's lifting.

We had only traveled a few hundred yards when Dick threw his arms in the air. Ann braked, and when I braked our bumpers hit. With the squeal of brakes, we disturbed the herd. As they scattered, I could see the main body of animals confronting us, and I knew why Dick was alarmed. The eland had been masking some massive buffalo. Buffalo have the reputation for being bold, sometimes savage animals. They were staring at us with small, beady eyes. Staring in a way which was nasty and distrustful, I thought. If they decided to attack, just one of the great animals could overturn our jeep.

I reached over and clutched Sheldon, whispering, "How much danger are we in?"

"We might be all right if we don't make any sudden moves," he said stroking my arm. "But keep the motor running." In a slow movement he kissed my hands and placed them back on the steering wheel, reminding me of my responsibility.

I wished that I wasn't the one who was driving. In a shaky voice I asked, "What should we do?"

Calmly, Sheldon said, "If I give you the signal, put her smartly into reverse, put your foot all the way down on the accelerator and back up into the trees."

"Shouldn't I turn around first?"

"There wouldn't be time, my darling," he replied. "But don't worry, my love, I really don't think they'll attack."

I caught my breath so as not to scream as, almost in a body, the huge buffalo lumbered toward us. I was about to ram the jeep into reverse, but Sheldon grabbed my arm, preventing me from doing so.

They only took a few steps forward and stopped. Several in the front rank raised their heads and sniffed the air. Then they turned, and the rest of the herd turned. Again as if in a body, they gathered a fair bit of speed and trotted off.

Turning over his shoulder to us, Dick said, "Just being cautious. I guess I've heard too many stories about the buffalo being the most dangerous animal in the bush."

"I think that's only when they're wounded," Sheldon called to him.

"I believe you're right," Dick called back. "But who the hell is willing to take the chance?"

Ann turned to me saying, "Wow, I didn't even see the buffalo until we were completely on top of them!"

"Neither did I!" I called back.

As Ann and I started out again, we both were giggling with relief.

In another hour of driving we had come upon a pride of lions. One of the five was an enormous black-maned one, always the most majestic-looking among the king of beasts. Evidently the pride had just eaten because the animals were dazed with weariness and kept closing their heavy-lidded, yellow eyes. We approached to within twelve or fifteen yards of them and they did nothing more than glance in our direction. Then the majestic black-maned one yawned widely, adding insult to our feelings of insignificance.

Altogether, the morning had been photographically disappointing for Ann and Dick. Staring buffalo and sleepy lions do not make exciting pictures, and they had hardly raised a camera. At eleven thirty we decided to find some shade where we could eat our sandwiches and rest for the next few hours. I spotted a wide-branched acacia near a small pack of zebra and headed toward it. I had motioned to Ann and she was following.

Just as I was about to pull under the tree, Sheldon dropped the binoculars, reached over and jerking the wheel, steered us straight toward the zebra pack. Once I'd braked, he handed me the binoculars, pointing to the tree. Ann had stopped and Dick was photographing something with a long telephoto lens.

Try as I might, I could see nothing but branches and thorns. Sheldon urged me to be patient and keep the binoculars trained on the lower right-hand side of the acacia. Moments passed in which I saw absolutely nothing. Then all at once, I registered a tiny movement, the slightest flick of a tail. Suddenly the thorns went out of focus and the leopard came into focus. It was like the experience of looking at an optical-illusion graphic. Widely separated thorns on a branch blended so completely with the tawny, black-spotted coat, that one either saw one or the other. It was a most remarkable camouflage.

We carefully checked out another tree and when it had been deemed free from big cats, both jeeps pulled in under its shade. After two close calls, first with the buffalo and then with the leopard, I felt like retiring permanently from behind the wheel of the Land Rover. That afternoon when we started out again, Sheldon drove our jeep and Dick took over from Ann.

In the latter half of the day we suddenly got lucky! As we were driving along a watercourse on the opposite side of the crater, we heard a deep roar and all at once a young lion, as yet maneless, rose up in front of us. About a hundred yards from the lion, a mixed herd of zebra and wildebeest were grazing. They stood very still, their heads turned to the lion. I had never witnessed this before and nobody had told me what was happening, but I instinctively knew. I experienced a sickly feeling in the pit of my stomach. The lion was on the hunt!

For the moment the lion seemed willing to play a waiting game. He sniffed at the breeze before slowly sinking onto his haunches. The herd nervously returned to their grazing. After several minutes he rose again, straight up in full view of his quarry. The zebra and wildebeest again froze at attention. Then the lion paced forward with slow and deliberate movements. The herd was still frozen in place. The lion growled. It was a terrifying sound. The herd bolted and I, myself, felt like making a fast getaway.

"Isn't that stupid!" I found myself shrieking. "I feel like running too! Why is he warning them? Doesn't he know that he'll frighten them off?"

"Those are his intentions exactly," Sheldon said. "You see that gully over there, where the herd is heading?"

"Yes."

"There will be a lioness waiting there."

"Oh, no!"

"His job is to drive the herd to her hiding place," he continued. "She's the one that will make the kill."

Sure enough the herd ran full out for a hundred yards or so and then turned, bewildered, to again face the stalking lion. The breeze had changed and they had smelled the lioness.

We stayed behind them as the Frasers circled around the scene. They stationed themselves just to the side of the lioness with a clear view of her and the distant herd. Ann and Dick frantically began checking to see that their camera equipment was ready. From a distance it looked as if cameras and lenses were flying from the back seat of the jeep, and they seemed to be slinging more and more things around their necks and over their shoulders. But once everything was ready, we had a very long wait ahead.

The lion carefully edged the herd forward but stopped short of rushing them into a movement which might veer them off course. The lioness, too, would not spring until she was certain of the nearness of her prey. It took two-and-a-half hours of nail-biting suspense. Then, in an instant, it was all over. I hadn't even seen the lioness as she crawled out of the gully on her belly. Suddenly she was crouched in the open only feet from the herd. And almost before I'd taken that in, she sprang and in one graceful arc bore the wildebeest to the ground, her teeth clamped into its throat.

The kill made, tension ceased and the scene returned to normal. It was as if nothing had happened. The herd even began to graze again, and quite near the felled wildebeest. The wildebeest and zebra ignored the carcass as though it were anything but one of their own, just killed.

The young male, who had merely a fringe where one day there would be a mane, tore a great slab of flank from the dead wildebeeste, while the lioness inched in slowly on her haunches so as not to rouse either the male's greed or his anger. Directly behind her two jackals were creeping, shielded from the male's sight by the lioness's crouching form. Three limping, whining hyenas made an outer circle and vultures slowly filled the branches of nearby trees.

That would be the order of the meal, the lineup of the diners: first the lion, then the lioness, followed by the jackals, hyenas, vultures, and finally the ants. However, it didn't always follow true to form; from time to time, one of the jackals would dart in and seize a tidbit out from under the lions' jaws. Often the hyenas would gang up on the jackal and force him to drop his stolen morsel. The vultures might try to get at what the lions had left before the hyenas had had their fill. Even the ants might ignore the fact that they were supposed to be last in line and arrive before the vultures had cleaned their share off the bones. If the ants got firmly entrenched on an unsuspecting vulture, they could turn him into the meal, devouring him alive in a matter of minutes. We did not stay for the entire drama of the eating because the Frasers already had photographed the afterkill.

We were out of the crater before sundown. It was cloudy again and just as we were pulling into camp the rain fell. It happened without warning, even before we had time to put the canvas tops on the jeeps, and we got soaked. I don't think any of us minded the rain, but Ann quickly climbed into the back of the jeep and threw herself over the film. As soon as Sheldon and Dick had parked, we got the roofs in place. While we were doing so, we were hit by sheets of daggerlike drops from above and speared from below by drops springing off the dry and rock-hard earth.

As the migration was over, many guests had checked out during the afternoon. Jove's was now only about one-quarter full. We were able to have an extra bucket of water for our showers, and the cocktail and dinner hours were less noisy occasions than they previously had been.

We were shown to a table on the roofed porch of the main building in case of more rain, but it never came. I was feeling a slight chill from having been wet and ordered a whiskey to have alongside my ale. Jove had shot a Grant's gazelle that day and we had for dinner what he called "a meal that sticks to the ribs": Grant's gazelle chops, green corn, and yams.

Ann and Dick could talk of nothing but the moment of the kill. It was just as well, I thought, because it diverted us from talking about the sad fact that this was their farewell dinner with us. Still, they wouldn't know the outcome of that one photographic moment until they were back in Vancouver and had looked at the developed film. They had been snapping all throughout the action but couldn't be sure if they had captured that split second as the lioness's teeth sank into the jugular.

"I know I got her spring," Ann said. "Her lunge was spectacular. It seemed prolonged to the point where I should have four or five frames of her almost suspended in air."

"And both you and Dick were photographing the same thing?" I asked.

"Yes."

"What are you worried about, then?"

"Well," Ann said, "the motors on the cameras just keep snapping the progression. All together the snaps will recreate an entire scene . . . each frame containing one of the individual seconds."

"Well, then you have the kill," I argued.

"Not necessarily," Dick said. "Or rather maybe yes, maybe no."

Ann tried to explain. "In a series of photos we will be able to give the impression of the kill . . . but we may not have that split second when the kill actually happened . . . when the teeth sank into the jugular."

"Forgive me," I said, "I don't understand why not."

"From years of movie making you of all people should understand film," Dick said.

"I don't understand a thing that goes on behind the camera," I confessed.

Both Ann and Dick looked at me as if it would be hopeless to continue. But Sheldon laughed and said, "Because, my darling, the shutter isn't continuously open, it blinks open and closed."

"And it might have closed its eye," I stated proudly, "just at that split second when the kill occurred!"

With that the three of them cheered and applauded. But they also insisted that it was up to me to buy a round of drinks, as punishment for having been so slow in comprehending.

Suddenly a long, slim, catlike thing darted with the speed of lightning up one wall, across the ceiling, and down the other wall, disappearing under the porch. Jove told us that it was a genet, a fast, tree-climbing creature related not to the cat but to the mongoose. The effect was startling, nonetheless, and it seemed there was scarcely a moment without some surprise.

The next morning around five we were forced to say good-bye to Ann and Dick. They were catching a plane for Nairobi at Sanya Juu airfield, near where the jeeps had been hired. Ann was driving their jeep and Dick was going to drive ours. Sheldon and I were heading in the opposite direction, planning to go into Uganda by boat. Ann and Dick had very kindly offered to return our jeep at the same time as they returned their own.

We all played at being jolly and keeping our chins up, but I'm certain that everyone felt a trifle weepy. The experiences we had been through together had soldered our friendship in a way that normally would have taken years. When we waved to Ann and Dick as they headed up the tarmac road back to Arusha, there was a large lump in my throat.

Jove had arranged for one of the Kikuyu who worked for him, a man named Shindi, to drive us to Mwanza where we could catch the steamer that crosses Lake Victoria into Uganda. We wanted to visit the Queen Elizabeth Game Park in Western Uganda, on its border with the Congo. The park had the largest herds of elephants to be found in East Africa. From Uganda we were hoping to cross into the Congo to try and catch sight of a tribe of pygmies who live in the mountains around Lake Kivu. Then we were flying back to Nairobi to reorganize for the next phase of our trip.

We wanted to get on the road for Mwanza directly after we had seen the Frasers off in order to catch the early steamer. We were in Jove's office saying good-bye when Shindi hurried in. Shindi, a tall, thin black man, was agitated and his Swahili words tumbled one over the other. Even his spindly legs seemed to be trembling beneath his khaki shorts.

Indeed it was a grave tale he had to tell. At the Masai village twenty miles west of Jove's, the watering hole had been poisoned by poachers. Scores of animals had died at its shores, their horns, tusks, and feet removed and the carcasses left. The group of Masai who had brought the news were in the courtyard asking for drinking water from Jove's well.

Jove instructed Shindi to fill the Masai's containers and then to fill some large barrels and place them in the Land Rover. Jove wanted to go to the Masai village himself and check out the situation, at the same time taking the village a supply of drinking water. He also wanted to prevent more death by taking dynamite, and with the Masai's permission, destroying the contaminated watering hole. I thought of what fury and despair Mac would have displayed at such a barbaric slaughter of game.

The village was on the way to Mwanza and Jove asked if we wished to go first with him to visit the Masai. Shindi would follow us in the other jeep. In case Jove got detained at the village, Shindi would proceed with us to the steamer's departure point.

Almost from the moment one enters East Africa, one begins to hear about the Masai or Ilmaasi, as they are called by all the maa-speaking peoples, which include the large tribes of the Samburu, Kawavi, and Arusha. They are also called Pastoral Masai by the white man, and they are proud seminomads who roam the great Rift Valley which stretches for miles across Kenya and Tanzania. Their god is Nagai and his home is the western summit of Kilimanjaro.

There are no chiefs, and each village, or manyatta, is run by a council of elders. The elders strongly adhere to traditional ways and resist cultural change, because a Masai feels himself to be an aristocrat, a member of a superior race.

He disdains all forms of trade or ordinary labor, and even his weapons are made for him by inferior tribes. Life for the Pastoral Masai revolves around their cattle, whom they believe were originally a divine gift from Nagai. Cattle represents their wealth, social position, and bartering power. They may keep a few sheep, goats, and pack donkeys, but a man needs cattle for every important transaction, such as bargaining for a wife.

The Ilmaasi religion tells them that Nagai divided the world not at the horizon, but below the surface of the earth so that everything on the surface is still one with the sky, and sacred. Everything below ground, however, is an unholy underworld, cursed by Nagai. The Masai will not disturb the underworld by digging in the soil to plant seeds, or even to bury their dead. The old are left out on the plains to be eaten by hyenas. Because a hut must be burned if someone dies in it, the sick also are taken into the bush, where they either recover and are brought back, or become too weak to fight off the carnivorous beasts.

The first sight of the members of a Masai tribe within their manyatta is a startling experience, perhaps because they are not at all like the other black Africans one sees. The men are at least six feet tall and some are as much as seven. They are slim-hipped, and stand straight as arrows. Their faces are long and thin with extremely high cheekbones, solidly good features, and large, well-defined noses. They have narrow slits for eyes, and look at strangers with arrogance and fierce pride.

Upon reaching manhood every young man is expected to kill a lion—alone and with only a spear. And each male carries one of

124

the treacherous-looking, long-bladed weapons at all times. The men wear nothing but a loosely draped, rust-colored cloak, which is knotted on one shoulder, and doesn't entirely cover their genitals. On occasion when I've been in close proximity to the men, I have experienced some difficulty in consciously averting my glance.

The Masai women are nearly as tall, but softer and rounder. Their bodies are scrupulously concealed in red-ochred cotton cloth, and married women are expected to identify themselves by shaving their heads.

Both men and women wear masses of beads and necklaces as well as metal armlets, bracelets, and leg bands. Their ears are pierced and then stretched fantastically with heavy ornaments.

Apparently the Masai never bathe, but I have found that they smell somewhat like musty straw and that the odor is not offensive. What does bother me is the way they permit flies to crawl freely over themselves and their children without making the least motion to shoo them away; there are always flies in their ears, eyes, mouths, and any open wounds.

We were with Jove in a typical Masai manyatta on the open plains. It was a stark camp, surrounded by a crude thornbush fence to protect the cattle at night, and within which they had built mud-and-dung huts shaped a bit like igloos. Cow dung dries quickly and keeps the air out of a shelter, so not only are Masai homes covered in dung; their campgrounds are paved in it as well. If you stand in one spot for too long, you find yourself sinking beneath the sunbaked crust and into the underlayer of moist excrement.

The cattle are a humped zebu type and most are poor, diseased specimens. While Jove held a meeting with the council of elders concerning the watering hole, Sheldon and I watched a Masai woman milk her cow. She then punctured a vein in its neck and drew off several cups of blood. She mixed the blood into the milk, and added a few drops of the cow's urine. On the spot I decided not to stay for lunch.

The mixture of milk, blood, and urine constitutes their entire diet. Only in times of great want are they permitted to eat the African staple, which is maize. The Masai warrior has the right at special times to substitute meat for his liquid diet, but he is bound to starve to death rather than allow vegetables or grain to pass his lips.

What their god demands of them seems to be unnecessarily harsh, and I have been horrified at the descriptions of their circumcision rites. It is a procedure which doesn't take place until the age of eleven, and is performed on both boys and girls. The ceremony is performed by the religious head of the tribe, or Oloiboni. It is done in the crudest possible way, and without concern for sanitary conditions.

Boys and girls circumcised at the same time are a separate group within the community. Initiated into adult life together, they are then eligible to marry only one another. A man may have more than one of these circumcision sisters as his wife, and he will not object to sharing his wives, so long as it is with circumcision brothers. But adultery outside the circle of coevals may be severely punished, even with death.

Masai peoples have become, over the years, less aggressive with strangers. The early explorers had found fierce warriors who fought one another, raided neighboring tribes, and murdered intruders. Many tales of horror had been told by the pioneers who had first penetrated their tribal areas. Even now whites who had been born in Kenya told stories about how the Masai once raided villages, first throwing spears, then cutting the throats of the men and boys with swords. Next came the slaughter of livestock, before they bludgeoned to death with wooden clubs the women and girls.

It seemed to Sheldon and me that even Jove was somewhat cautious in his dealings with the Masai. He sat on the ground for an hour with the old men of the tribe, drinking honey beer with them and explaining the need to dynamite the watering hole so as to disperse the poisoned water. Jove, like Mac, was a state ranger and did not need the Masai's permission, but he had too much respect for the peoples of the land to ignore their feelings and too much sense to incur their wrath.

Ironically, in the end it was Jove, as well as the poachers, who would be responsible for the death of a Masai warrior. Sheldon and I already had gone and only heard the story second-hand from Mac. Mercifully, we had been well on our way to Mwanza when the tragedy occurred.

Once the watering hole had been packed with dynamite and the fuse set, everyone retreated to behind a distant mound. Unbeknownst to Jove or the others, one of the warriors had arrived from a journey and had knelt to refresh himself at the very moment the blast went off.

Jove had gone to the Masai village with only the best of intentions, to render the spot harmless and save the natives and animals from the poisoned water. The Masai tribe took no retribution for the death, but it seems that Jove could never forgive himself.

Man, intentionally and unintentionally, is truly what Mac had called us: "The Great Destroyers."

As for the slain Masai, he never realized that there was a danger from the poison or explosives. It was an altogether ignoble way for a brave warrior to die. At least, as a boy, when he had marched out alone with only a spear to face that lion, he had been able to pit his skills against his enemy and make choices. But then, he had confronted an animal he understood.

TOP: Witnessing the migration across the Serengeti plains is a once-in-a-lifetime experience. Here the buffalo was part of the long stampede.
Photo credit: Enrico Mandel-Mantello

ABOVE: On the plains of the Serengeti one quickly learns to examine the overhead branches before parking under a tree. Can you spot the leopard?
BELOW: This leopard is easier to see. *Photo credit: Enrico Mandel-Mantello*

ABOVE: We stopped at a Masai village on our way to Uganda. Here, a Masai mother with her child—note the fly burrowing into the baby's face.

BELOW: To prove his manhood and become a warrior, a Masai boy must go into the bush alone and kill a lion with a spear.

CHAPTER TWELVE

We arrived at the Lake Victoria steamer in time for the noon sailing. Rainclouds had been gathering all morning and moments before the gangplank was raised, the sky turned black. We had barely left shore when the downpour came with such force that Sheldon and I were convinced the rainy season had begun.

However, this was not the real thing. It lasted perhaps half an hour before vanishing without a trace, and we were to have clear blue skies for our entire stay in Uganda. In fact, the next morning we awoke far out in the lake to see one of the most dazzling sunrises either of us ever had witnessed: a double image of the sky, divided at the horizon, reflected with complete clarity in the smoothness of the lake's surface.

When we disembarked in Bukoba, we immediately became aware of a difference in attitude among the people. Unlike

Kenya or Tanzania, Uganda seemed to be sluggish, suspended in a state of uncertainty. We were hard-pressed to find a taxi or bus to the tourist office, and when we did reach the office the staff was of little help in recommending a lodge near the Queen Elizabeth Park or even finding us the address of a jeep rental firm.

Torn by diverse tribal and political factions, Uganda had been a trouble spot of British East Africa. Tensions had increasingly worsened since the 1962 independence from Great Britain, and many felt that from that point, treachery was on a runaway course. During Milton Obote's long term in office as prime minister he had ministers who disagreed with him arrested; he suspended the Constitution; and he had sent soldiers to burn the palace of the Kabaka of Buganda. With these gross miscarriages of justice, the country reverted to a state of martial law.

By January, 1971, Idi Amin already had taken control of the government by means of a military coup. When we arrived in Uganda in February, he had thus far assassinated only political opposition, and was still being supported by both the British and the Americans. His ten-year reign of terror was yet to come to full prominence. However, early in his takeover there was a sense of doom. Discomforting rumors abounded daily and many individuals in positions of responsibility were leaving the country, increasing the growing number of abandoned schools, churches, hospitals, and businesses.

The disorganization we found was the reason why it was late in the day before we managed to accomplish a few simple things such as hire a jeep, find a road map, and get the name of a lodge near the park. The roads were bumpy and in disrepair, there were almost no service stations, and we kept seeing broken-down vehicles left by the roadside to rust. Despite a lack of road signs, we managed to find the lodge but then we were in for a nasty surprise. At one end of the grounds there were several dilapidated tents and at the other end, a temporary construction office where a black man and woman were living and acting as overseers. In between were the bungalows of the incomplete development, left midway through their construction.

Apparently many stranded travelers passed this way, and the couple were in the habit of renting tents and providing a bath and a meal. They seemed genuine in their unawareness of any nearby operational lodge, and as it would be dark soon, we didn't dare chance searching for other accommodations.

I chose one of the tents which seemed to be in fairly good repair and Sheldon unloaded the luggage from the jeep. Our suitcases were lined up by the side of the tent and I had meant to bring them inside after the woman and I had made it presentable and put linen and blankets on the camp beds. It took a long time to ready the tent, however, and once finished I stopped to have a whiskey-and-soda, completely forgetting about the luggage.

The man had set up a small bar and built a campfire. He also had placed near the fire a large round tub made of tin to serve as a bath, and while Sheldon and I sipped our whiskey-and-sodas, the couple transported bucket after bucket of hot water from their far-distant stove.

When the tub was full, the man told us that dinner would be served to us in one hour's time, and then he and the woman disappeared down the long path toward the construction office where they lived.

It was a rather mild evening on the lush green plains. The woman had left us two large bath towels, and I got from my shoulder bag a cake of soap in a plastic container.

Perhaps Sheldon and I were meant to take turns in the tub but there was no question of that. We stripped and climbed in together. Bathing in the open, beside a campfire and under a full moon was an exhilarating experience which sent tingles of expectancy through me. The night was so beautiful that we lay back in the water, sipping our drinks and observing the stars. Only when the water turned cold did we wash quickly and get out to dry.

Sheldon had unpacked two caftans and we each slipped one on, then sat with our arms around one another by the fire until we felt warm again. We knew that we were just south of the Ruwenzori range and the Mountains of the Moon, but we could see no peaks. From where we were the entire earth appeared to be flat. We speculated that it was little wonder in such a setting that our ancient forefathers believed if you traveled far enough you would simply drop off the edge.

Our tent was perhaps four or five hundred yards from the shore of a lake where the mimosa trees grew more closely together than they did on the rest of the plain. As we stared out toward the lake, we saw moving among the trees some barrel-shaped animals with short legs. Now and again we caught a glimpse of their horn noses silhouetted in the moonlight, and knew them to be rhinoceroses.

The chorus of frogs and crickets was almost deafening, but several times beneath their songs we heard the low bass notes of a lion's growl.

This was one habitat of the rare tree-climbing lion. An old male, who no longer lived with the pride, resided in the branches of a tree on the lakefront facing us. Apparently, he was too old to hunt and lived mostly on small rodents.

As he served us our stew, the black man told us of how the pathetic old simba sometimes strolled into camp to rummage through the garbage cans. He said that in times when hunters left an abundance of game, he would take it upon himself to deliver a carcass, leaning it just below the tree home of the old simba.

After the black man and his wife retired for the night, I felt a foreboding about our being alone in this deserted spot, where a lion was in the habit of searching for food, while we only were to have a canvas tent as protection. I wished that I had some kind of weapon, a small handgun plus, of course, the ability to use it.

It occurred to me that perhaps we would be better off sitting up all night and keeping the fire going. Or perhaps we could take turns being lookout.

My attention was focused on the trees of the nearby lake from where the lonely lion emitted prolonged, mournful sounds.

A breeze stirred, as if in response to the lion's cries, and the flames in front of us rose, throwing sparks to the sky. Sheldon rose straight up from his place, staring at the lake.

I was more bewildered than alarmed, because it was a bright moonlit plain and I could see nothing to threaten us.

"What is it, darling?" I whispered.

"I'm dying," he choked, throwing his arms above his head and beginning to tremble.

I began to call for help but the construction office was too far away for the black couple to hear me.

All at once Sheldon grew very still. Then his body stiffened and he slumped to the ground, saliva coming from his mouth.

I had never witnessed an epileptic attack, and it shocked me. I didn't know what to do for *grand mal.* I had heard somewhere that those afflicted must not be allowed to swallow their tongues, so I searched for something to use, found a stick, and forced it between his jaws.

Then he became motionless. Gazing into the fire, I sat rocking him in my arms.

When he came round there was a fleeting hostility in his look before he focused on my face and his expression softened, and then a new confusion set in. Sheldon did not want to talk about the experience. It had left him exhausted, and he wanted me to show him where we were sleeping. I took his hand and led him through the tent opening. He groped for one of the cots, threw himself on it and slurred the words: "I'm sorry, darling," just before passing into a deep slumber.

I sat beside the fire, adding wood to it until the pile of extra kindling was gone. I did not want to venture out alone to gather wood. Walking out in the plains alone was asking for trouble. If there was to be an all-night vigil, it had to be done by two people, so while one might be occupied at some task, the other could remain watchful.

Not only did I feel drained after Sheldon's attack, but it had happened at the end of an altogether trying day. I looked in every direction and nothing was stirring anywhere near us. I reasoned that my imagination no doubt was overactive and that in all probability we were perfectly safe here. So I entered the tent, pulled down the zipper to seal the flap, and dropped wearily onto the cot next to the one that held the deeply sleeping Sheldon.

I was restless and slept only in fits. I don't know how much time passed but at one moment I sat up and saw that the fire was no longer making shadows on the tent, and I wished I had not permitted it to die out. Sheldon still was sleeping soundly and I, too, felt very, very tired. Again, I drifted.

Growls disrupted my sleep, emerging from my dreams and surrounding my waking state. Something was just outside the canvas walls and moving back and forth, in a crescent.

I was certain it was the lion, pacing in a semicircle, getting ready to rip through the tent to make a meal of us.

There was no time to plan my reaction—I behaved purely on instinct. My mind told me that I could not bear the slow agonizing suspense before the kill. Obviously I was going to die, so I wanted it to be swift. I wanted to face death head on and have it be done. With fingers trembling so that I could barely grip the zipper pull, I tore open the tent and flung myself outside.

There was an overwhelming, putrid smell. Something smaller than a lion yet nearly as big as I humped away. At the same time an inanimate object fell with a thud to the ground in front of me. It was my suitcase.

Coming from the other side of the tent were terrifying growls made by more than one animal. I steeled myself and took a few steps around to where I could see.

Clearly visible in the moonlight were three hyenas, the brown ones larger than any dog. They were wrenching, ripping, and tearing at Sheldon's suitcase, and threatening each other over possession of the leathery meal.

What creature is more hideous than the hyena, who preys on the young, the weak, and the dying, but who is in fact capable of anything including, when wounded, eating his own entrails? If they were sufficiently hungry, the hyenas posed as much danger as the lion. If they had not eaten for a considerable time, they would have been daring enough to circle me, dart at me from different directions, and snatch pieces of my flesh.

They hesitated. With distorted bodies they peered at me over humped shoulders. Seething with hatred, they were deciding whether to attack, openly threatening me, testing my willingness to be a victim. They stretched enormous jaws exposing blades of teeth, and the sounds they directed at me might have come straight from the depths of hell.

I did what desperate animals often do when trapped—I bluffed. Beside me I found a metal washbasin and a spoon that had fallen to the ground. I picked them up and beat the washbasin for all I was worth. At the same time, I screeched with a fury born of terror and rushed at them.

They fled, and at first I thought it was solely because they had accepted my bluff. However, when I turned, I saw that Sheldon was by my side holding a club. The heavy stick had been one of those stretching the canvas of his cot. He had slept through the noise of the hyenas, but my shrieks had pierced his unconscious.

We collected what remained of our luggage and took it inside. My case, which had been dropped in front of me by the first fleeing hyena, had no handles, and the leather trim had been eaten. Sheldon's case had caused the fight among them because it was made

entirely of leather. Now less than two-thirds of it remained, rendering it quite useless.

We were able to laugh at the nature of the scare, but nonetheless
we rebuilt the fire and sat up for what remained of the night,
finishing off the bottle of whiskey.

At the first hint of dawn, we were on our way in the general
direction of the Queen Elizabeth Park, and this day favored us
much more than had the day before. We had traveled only twenty
miles or so when we came upon a comfortable, well-run lodge, just
outside the park gates.

We registered and were shown to an invitingly cool bungalow
nestled among mimosa. Although we were most anxious to view
the elephants that we had traveled to Uganda to see, when we
entered the bedroom and saw and felt the luxurious white bed, we
could not resist a peaceful sleep. Just this one morning, the tracking
of elephants could wait.

Sheldon and I wasted no time undressing. Standing on either
side of the large bed, we jointly folded back the topsheet together
with the white chenille spread.

The undersheet was tautly pulled over a firm mattress and it was
made of smooth linen which, when we lowered our bodies onto
the bed, fairly caressed the skin. My muscles ached, and I stretched
and yawned and moaned with the pleasure of such comfort. Then
I snuggled into Sheldon's waiting arms, where we rolled and
stretched and moaned together. When we ceased roaming the bed,
we made a nearly soundless, almost motionless love, which transported us from relaxed euphoria to tranquil dreams.

Around noon we awakened ourselves by the same method we
had used to help ourselves to sleep, by making love.

After a shower and some lunch, we were ready to pursue our
quest of elephants. Although there was always a certain amount
of risk with Sheldon behind the wheel, I never objected to his
driving in open country. As I had driven our jeep that morning, it

was he who drove us to the park, and what a lovely drive it was! This was a beautiful rolling countryside with lakes in every direction and although we were there at the height of the dry season, everything looked abundantly rich and green.

At the entrance to the park, we passed under a stone archway where the word *Equator* was inscribed. Beside the arch a yellow road sign read:

QUEEN ELIZABETH NATIONAL PARK
ELEPHANTS
HAVE
RIGHT OF WAY

Indeed we had traveled only a short distance before a huge congregation of elephants crossed the road a few hundred feet in front of us. At first we were panic-stricken by their size and numbers. Then we forgot our fear and became absorbed in watching them.

With four hundred or so elephants ahead of us, we understood that this must be more than one herd, that it was a congregation of herds. There were so many animals that it took at least a quarter of an hour for them to cross. When they moved out into the open country, we decided to follow behind them, keeping a safe distance, of course. They didn't seem to be taking any notice of us. Elephants' vision and hearing are quite poorly developed. They have a keen sense of smell, but the gasoline fumes would have camouflaged us. So long as we didn't get too close or leave the jeep, we would be perfectly safe. Anyway elephants rarely attack. The time to watch your step is if you see their ears fan out like sails!

I wanted to get a look at the babies, some of which seemed only to be three feet high, but they were being sheltered. There was no question of those stumbling babies being trampled in the crush, because the adults always note and inspect a newborn calf and then carefully look after it as if it were their own.

We were on a sloping green hillside which led down to a distant lake (Lake Edward, I believe), and the herds seemed headed in its direction. The trek was slow, as they were uprooting bushes and trees as they went, eating the roots and rejecting the rest. At other times of the year they would eat only the leaves or only the stems; this was the time to eat roots. As these largest of land mammals feed for some nineteen hours a day and weigh on an average of six tons, it made me wonder if choosing their diet so carefully was not nature's plan for the survival of the vegetation. Later I was to discover that certain trees have to be uprooted in order to seed.

Sheldon said that there were no bulls among the huge congregation. Although many of the males looked to be adult, they don't breed until eighteen or twenty years of age, and they are not fully grown until they reach twenty-five. The mature males live apart and only return when a female is in season.

Each herd is led by a matriarch, and it is her knowledge and judgment which determines the survival of the herd, just as her sisters and daughters will lead their herds and be responsible for their survival. The herds would have been separated throughout the dry season, going their individual ways in search of food. Now reaffirming family ties, they were congregating for this reunion. A congregation such as the one we were witnessing was a sure sign that the rainy season was close at hand.

The coming rains would profoundly affect Sheldon and me: our trip would be at an end, and from then on . . . our life together.

CHAPTER THIRTEEN

During our first afternoon in the Queen Elizabeth Park, we followed the congregation of elephants as far as the lake, but because we were afraid of getting lost after dark we had hurried back to the lodge as soon as the sun began to set. I believe that even Sheldon, who disliked being with groups, would have wished for more tourists to be present. We had not seen another car all that day and, what was more troubling, no guides or rangers.

That evening as we parked the car and walked toward the bungalow, we saw our houseboy, Ashti. We had met Ashti only briefly when we had checked into the lodge. Now he was sitting on his heels below the steps of our front porch, waiting for us to return.

He was a frail, timid Indian man, who seemed to speak very seldom, and then only in broken sentences. *"Jambo,* bwana. *Jambo,* memsahib,"* he greeted us as he rose and bowed. He was dressed in a faded blue smock and loose trousers, and a pair of sandals which we later learned had been carved out of an old rubber tire.

Inside we saw that he had set a side table with a red cloth on top of which he had placed a tray of fruit, biscuits, and a steaming pot of green tea. It looked like a sufficient meal and we thought about skipping dinner in the dining room. However, Ashti handed us a note from the manager, a Dr. Mbowa, requesting that we join him for a meal that evening.

Sheldon said, "*Mwema,* ('good') Dr. Mbowa, *asante* ('thank him very much') *Naam* ('yes')." And Ashti bowed and went to deliver our acceptance. I had to laugh at such a terse reply, but the tourist Swahili books consist of a limited vocabulary and a few idioms.

Sheldon sat down in an easy chair by the fire that Ashti had built sometime earlier, and motioned for me to sit on his lap. I did, but first I poured us both a cup of the aromatic green tea, which was just the thing to have at the end of a thirsty afternoon. In fact, while everything had seemed lusciously green, February was the hottest, driest month of the year in Western Uganda. The elephants had kicked up so much dry dirt and dust that sometimes it had veiled them in what looked like a smokescreen. I was still feeling the dryness in my nose and throat, and the tea was welcome.

While we had been gone that day, Ashti had attended to our lacerated suitcases and unpacked our jumbled garments. Even before the hyenas had sent everything flying, I had begun to feel an urgent need for some clean clothes. I was delighted to see what Ashti had done: everything in our limited wardrobes had been laundered. Our outer garments had been brushed and pressed, and even our boots and shoes had been polished. As we had clean clothes for a change, we decided to dress for dinner, something we hadn't done since our evenings at Tsavo.

When we walked into the dining hall, I was glad that Sheldon was wearing a clean white shirt, neatly pressed gray trousers, and a navy jacket, and that I was wearing a dress rather than trousers. The black gentleman who rose and introduced himself as Dr. Mbowa was impeccably groomed. For us to have been dressed ultra-casually might have seemed an affront to him.

I was somewhat uncertain as to how I should behave in the presence of our black African host. Sheldon, however, didn't seem to know the meaning of the word *different* in its application to other human beings, and he was his usual natural self. And Richard Mbowa was much less self-conscious about his relationship with us than I might have feared. In fact, he seemed so charming and relaxed that I was soon put at my ease.

Richard Mbowa had been schooled in Great Britain and was a well-educated, refined, idealistic man. Rather than seeking wealth in the outside world, he had returned to Africa to bring his knowledge and ability home to his own peoples.

Richard apologized for the present government of Uganda and the state of things in general in black Africa, as though such matters were solely his responsibility.

"It is very sad, what is happening in my country," he told us, "but we one day will have to adjust to these new times. Then hopefully we can invite back the large non-African population Uganda once attracted. Oh, I do not simply mean the Europeans. We once had many more Indo-Pakistani and Arabs. Also, our tribes will have to learn to live together, at least in civility if not in complete harmony."

He paused here, but Sheldon and I were interested to hear his point of view and he soon continued: "We have broken the yoke of colonialism, although admittedly it had taught us many valuable things. It is as if we have to demolish its teachings before we can go back and pick up the threads of what it had given us of worth. I hope only that in this terrible transitional period we are not set upon again by a much subtler master who would enslave us. I fear those who hide their evil under a banner of socialism."

We asked him if he intended to go into politics but he said he had not thought seriously in that direction. He had graduated from Cambridge only six months before and returned to manage the lodge, as his father had done before his retirement. Richard was presently in the process of buying the property from its previous European owners by means of a profit-sharing arrangement. He was also interested in keeping up the nearby cotton plantation where his grandparents had spent their lives. Thanks to the British policy of agricultural trade development, Uganda had enjoyed a good cotton export business.

Richard seemed distressed over the fact that there were so few guests at the moment and so few people employed at the Queen Elizabeth Game Park, as well as at his lodge. It was apparently the fashion for Bantu peoples to shun employment, a fad which Richard fervently hoped would pass.

We assured him of our confidence that any tourists who did stay at his lodge would without fail recommend it to their friends. Sheldon and I certainly had every intention of doing so. We admitted that we had been a bit concerned at the lack of supervision at the park, but we could find no fault with the hotel service. In fact, our houseboy, Ashti, was a jewel.

Houseboy definitely had been the wrong thing to say. Richard remained polite but there was a fiery glint in his eyes as he said, "Yes, but we must breed no more houseboys. We want workers who are equal because they do their jobs well."

Then he paused and looked rather sad. "Our people must stop looking for something for nothing, stop believing those who tell them that they will have material wealth whether or not they earn it. That is deceitful and truly evil."

Our bungalow was only a short distance from the main building, but Richard would not allow us to walk and insisted on driving us to our front door.

As he drove us he said, "With so few people about, the animals are daring about entering the compound. The lake is close by and a stray hippo often passes this way. As a boy, when I could not sleep and used to sit looking out my bedroom window, I remember seeing them in our backyard."

Sure enough, he braked at that moment as one of the giant river horses swayed in front of the car.

Richard asked us if we were going to take the launch across the lake in the morning, and we said that we were.

"That is where you will see all the tourists from near and far gathered. It is great good fun being out on the lake with the hippos swimming around you. We have here in the lakes of the park the greatest concentration of hippopotami in existence."

There was something sad and brave, touching and admirable about Richard in his somewhat solitary struggle. As we said good-night, I reached over and kissed him on the cheek. "You don't know how much I admire you, Richard," I said, "and how much I wish you well."

"That's right, old man," Sheldon said. "We are rooting for you all the way. We'll do our damned best to send some guests your way."

"That is fine, thank you," Richard said. Then he shook Sheldon's hand and kissed mine, saying: "Perhaps one day you will come back for a return visit, when the lodge is full. I know in my heart that the Bantu peoples will return to work one day soon. Then there will be a real chance for all of us to have prosperity."

One of the most enjoyable sights during our stay in East Africa was seeing the hippos. I'm not exactly sure why, but hippos came to hold an interest for me in a way that exceeded my interest in any of the other animals.

Certainly the best way to see them is to take the launch along the lakes. Protruding eyes and nostrils stay above the water, while the animals float with the rest of their bodies submerged. As the launch proceeds, all around at the surface of the water there are eyes watching. Huge, watery eyes that look for a moment and then vanish.

I got the distinct impression that the hippos were playing games with Sheldon and me and the other tourists on board.

Moments after the hippos disappeared, the surface would be perfectly still. They can remain underwater for a considerable length of time. Then, in various places, a small telltale line of bubbles would float to the top. Suddenly one of the big river horses would rise up so close to the edge of the flat-bottomed boat that you could, if you were fast enough, reach out and touch it.

In a matter of seconds others were popping up until the launch was surrounded by the big fellows.

Often there were thirty, forty, sometimes even fifty at one time. They would all be under the launch, swim underwater, or walk along the bottom until reaching the side of the boat, then rise and salute us with spouts of water.

Presumably our flat-bottomed and open launch was heavy, but I felt sure that a group of forty or fifty animals of that size could have overturned us, had they been so inclined.

The big prehistoric beasts seemed to be putting on a show for us. And I wasn't alone in my cries of delight. Men and women alike were squealing in their astonishment, so surprised were they at the hide-and-seek aspect of the play, as well as the way the hippos would suddenly pop up directly in front of us. Very few of us managed to take even one worthwhile photograph, we were so involved in their spirited games.

There was one moment when I was certain that all the hippos had swum to the opposite shore. I was gazing into the muddy water, chin on railing, daydreaming, when all at once a gigantic head broke through the surface only inches from me. It flicked its pointy ears and spouted water straight up from his nostrils. Then it opened its mouth wide enough to swallow me. I dissolved into laughter when instead I heard, "Moo."

That short, deep monosyllabic *moo* accompanied by grunts greeted us all up and down the lakes. The hippos on shore seemed to be having conversations. A colony of fifty or sixty would be wallowing in the mud along the shallows. The sight of these big blubbery creatures, completely caked in mud as thick as the African gumbo, sliding helplessly and wallowing even on top of one another in their clumsiness, was for me wonderfully comic.

The males are said to be aggressive during the breeding season and sometimes the contests are fatal. A few of the ones we saw were covered with scars. A few even had fresh wounds about the back and shoulders. But I put this down mostly to their awkwardness, rather than to a great deal of discord.

At times they roared in pairs out of the water, met head on, and had a contest, it seemed to me, to see which one could open its jaws the widest. There were people around us who claimed these were battles, others that they were signs of lovemaking. Perhaps it was a bit of both, but I looked on it as just more of their spirited hijinks.

It is true that they smell a bit like open drains, and that most of the day they appear to be nothing short of indolent. Still, I developed a special fondness for them, perhaps because I sensed that they were quite capable of demolishing us, but preferred instead to share with us their playful antics.

Most of the time, hippos lie close to the surface of the water, gently submerging and rising again, as if existence itself were sufficient reason for being. And indeed, wasn't that the overwhelming message one received in Africa? Here one became aware of survival as the only essential achievement. And, yes, that the reason for being was to exist.

Sheldon gently shook me out of my reverie to show me two bull elephants on the shore. They were truly magnificent, with a quality of timeless nobility. They had been on earth long before man and yet how terrible to reflect that they were in danger of extinction, and probably within my lifetime.

A little further on a herd of elephants were splashing. They were spraying themselves and each other in continual showers. One thought that perhaps they might empty the lake. Each one drinks as much as five bathtubs full of water per day. We watched them swinging gallons from trunk to mouth. Some were rolling in the mud of the bank or splashing in the shallows and throwing the water far enough to start another watering hole. From the launch I had a clear view of the babies, tripping themselves and their playmates, under the loving and watchful eyes of the adults.

If attentive enough, one could see every animal in the reserve. Sooner or later they all came to the lake to drink. We watched a cheetah lapping the water with its bright pink tongue while glancing in all directions and being extremely cautious. One wondered which enemy it was cowering from. There couldn't be many creatures it feared. Perhaps only us, the humans—the great destroyers.

A little further along, a rhino came to drink, dispersing in the process a gathering of male elephants. The rhino is the only animal in the bush capable of injuring a fully grown elephant, and while they didn't run, they nonetheless showed the rhino due respect by allowing it a clear path to the lake.

Further on we saw another comic scene which made us laugh. While one baboon was drinking, a larger one came along, lifted it by the scruff of its neck, flung it aside and assumed its spot on the bank. It was an outrageous act because with all that wide expanse of lakefront, why insist on that very spot? I suppose we laughed because it was behavior not dissimilar to that of human children.

We'd had some refreshments on the launch and instead of going back to the lodge for our siesta, we decided to stretch out on top of a grassy knoll overlooking the lake. By borrowing Sheldon's camera, I was able to take a photograph of him which is one of my favorites. It is of him in profile, sitting on top of that hill which slopes down to the lake, where a lone bull elephant stands by the shore.

It was particularly lovely on the knoll, and we felt reasonably safe sleeping in the open during the heat of the day, when all else slept as well. However, if there had been rangers on guard, they never would have permitted us to leave the jeep.

That day I saw my first baobab tree. My introduction to that astounding tree with its fantastic buttresses had been in the book *The Little Prince,* which I had read as a child. I'm not sure I believed that they existed outside of the little prince's fantasy. But now I was actually able to touch one and, again borrowing Sheldon's camera, take a photograph of that most massive of trees.

It was a breezeless, excruciatingly hot day and the plains were swathed in shimmering heat late into the afternoon. As I was driving us back to the lodge, we passed a wooded area where there were some elephants asleep standing up. Sheldon wanted to get some pictures and he kept coaxing me to drive closer and closer. In an instant, even as he woke, the big bull closest to us fanned his ears! I threw the jeep into reverse, convinced that the big fellow would be in hot pursuit. But thanks to the terrible heat of that airless day, he was reluctant to charge and we escaped without incident.

That evening we attempted to telephone the hospital in Nairobi to find out about Cathy and Susan. But after a six-hour wait, we gave up. We decided to go into the Congo as soon as the arrangements could be made, and then instead of spending the rest of the week in Uganda, we felt we should go back to Nairobi. Since we had been so lucky in seeing the animals of Uganda, we didn't feel we needed the extra time.

ABOVE: Two signs that greeted us at the entrance of the Queen Elizabeth Park.

ABOVE: I was so scared photographing this elephant at such close range that my finger slipped into the right corner of the frame.

LEFT: Feeling very brave, Sheldon and I observed the elephants for a while from this grassy knoll in Queen Elizabeth Park. There were no guards around, and few tourists.

ABOVE: Elephants rarely attack, but the time to watch your step is when their ears fan out like sails. *Photo credit: Enrico Mandel-Mantello*

LEFT: We were able to observe a wide assortment of animals at the lake, since sooner or later they all came to drink. Here is a water buffalo quenching its thirst. Crocodiles abound in this area as well.

BELOW: In our flat-bottomed boat we were sometimes surrounded by a herd of forty or fifty hippos at a time.

CHAPTER FOURTEEN

Richard Mbowa had arranged for a bodyguard and driver named Kaufe to take us in his car into the Congo. Somewhere across the border a French Congolese tourist official was to join us as guide to the pygmy village.

Because of the political upheaval and high instance of crime in the Congo, Richard had urged us not to go on our own: "Kaufe is an African and an ex-army major. He will be carrying a rifle as well as a handgun. One needs to take a great deal of precaution these days," he said. "Besides," he added with a grin, "things are very slow in the tourist business and my friend Kaufe can certainly use the work." He had returned once more to a serious note. "Wealthy-looking whites driving on isolated roads are perfect prey for bandits. Border guards who might be tempted to confiscate your money and vehicle will be less likely to risk it if Kaufe is driving you. When you meet him you will appreciate what I mean."

Indeed, the first sight of our driver left Sheldon and me a bit speechless. Kaufe was Somalian; a most impressive, haughty and regal representative of his race. His skin glowed like polished blue ebony. He was tall and gaunt with long, straight legs showing beneath a khaki tunic. Seeing an ex-army officer in a tunic might have appeared odd to us, but the tunic draped from Kaufe's slim, erect torso like some regal vestment.

He wore a distinguished patch over one eye where he had lost its sight in an attack by the dreaded spitting cobra, and he carried a rifle as though it were a scepter. But we were never tempted to think of him in terms of merely a picturesque figure. His rare smile resembled a sneer and his teeth, when thus exposed, were akin to those of a wolf. Kaufe was more usually somber, with little to say. Even as chauffeur, he apparently found no need to apologize for the bumpy ride we were having on the springless backseat of his ancient Chevrolet.

To this day, it remains the most dreadful automobile ride I have ever experienced. Our acute discomfort was not exclusively caused by the asthmatically choking old car which chugged us along. Once we were heading through the jungle, everything about the trip seemed to contribute its share in equal measure. Certainly the dirt roads were the roughest imaginable as they were of baked mud, broken endlessly in ridges and deep potholes. There was not a hint of a breeze for the entire three hour jungle drive. To add to our misery, Sheldon and I had smeared ourselves from head to foot in an insect-repellent oil. This was the home of the malaria-carrying mosquito and the tsetse fly, which transmits sleeping sickness. We sweltered in intense heat, with what must have been a 99.99 percent humidity under a sickly yellow-soup sky. There were many times when I thought seriously of suggesting that we turn back.

Everything in this part of Equatorial Africa looked to be smothered in dense vegetation under a thick canopy of trees. Even the border post, which turned out to be deserted, was overgrown and nearly hidden from view. We could see nothing that lived inside that massive foliage unless it ventured onto our hacked-out trail. Yet this was the country where it was possible to see gigantic wild boar and small pygmy elephants. To the northeast lived the white rhinoceros, and high in the mountains the gorilla made its last sad stand.

We did get a fleeting glance at a family of chimpanzee as they swung across the road on ropelike vines, or lianas. We also witnessed that day the hideous sight of an anaconda, or python, or boa constrictor stretched across our path. I am not alone in my confusion over the name of these monsters. They are all of related subfamilies within the family of *Boidae*, therefore I shall simply refer to it as a boa.

We had come upon it quite suddenly, and as it was so thick and long, at first I had assumed it to be a felled tree trunk. When we braked in front of it I saw the patterns of brown, tan and yellow arranged in diamond shapes and knew it to be one of those snakes that kill their prey by constriction before swallowing them whole.

The boa was draped from a high tree branch at one side of the road and stretched across the width of the road, working its way into another high tree at the opposite side. It was at least thirty feet long and as every inch of that immense, nightmare-inducing reptile slithered by, I felt as if my own flesh were crawling.

Finally we had crossed into Kivu Province and were heading in the general direction of Rutshuru, at the foot of the mountains near Lake Kivu. The Congo was one of the more sparsely populated countries in Africa, and during most of the jungle drive toward Rutshuru we saw no other human beings.

Then all at once the road widened and we came upon a vision of loveliness walking down it. She was a Mangbetu woman with a cone-shaped hat and the features of the ancient Egyptian queen, Nefertiti. Among the Congo's two hundred different tribes are to be found some of the world's most breathtakingly beautiful people, interbred from the tribes of not only Egypt, but the Sudan and much further afield. During our short stay we saw voluptuous girls with caffè-latte skin who were dressed in woven bark, and exotic girls who looked like Abyssinian cats and dressed in animal skins.

There were several reasons for the wide variety of peoples to be found in the Congo. The former Belgian Congo, known when we were there in 1971 as the Democratic Republic of the Congo, lies in a central position in Africa and borders with ten other countries. Its rich lumber, rubber, and extremely varied mineral wealth attracts eager prospectors, and its extensive waterways, supplemented by railroads, make it eminently accessible.

Within the country, the tributaries of the Nile and Congo rivers must number in their thousands. Yet they are not the only valuable commercial waterways. There are many lakes, the largest being Tanganyika, Kivu, Edward, and Albert. And the country stretches in the west all the way to the Atlantic Ocean, where it has ports, the waters of which are deep enough for ocean steamers.

But it is not a place where many prospectors chose to settle. It seems they skimmed away natural resources while leaving behind the seed of their offspring in native wombs. In all fairness I should say that much of the mountains, rain forests, and jungles are savagely hostile to man. Even as late as the nineteen-seventies there were vast areas which had not been explored, and that probably holds true to this day.

We passed through some farming country where we witnessed the local people carrying out their day-to-day routines. In fields the women wore clumps of freshly gathered leaves attached to a thong around their waists and the men wore nothing at all. Not a single person appeared to be idle. Young boys had bales of fire-wood or straw on their heads, and young girls carried gourds of water. Each woman we saw had on her back a baby riding in a sling, and those bobbing heads looked at us with big, startled eyes.

We came to the foothills of the Mountains of the Moon and found the marketplace where we were supposed to meet our guide. The people of the town knew almost nothing of tourists. The goods they had to sell were for local consumption: maize, sorgo, peas, and beans. There were no stalls; each vendor simply spread a piece of cotton cloth on the ground on which to display bananas or rice, feathers or beads, fish or rodents.

They seemed to love beads and beaded ornaments, and the townspeople wore flowing robes of brilliant hues. Here and there a more affluent merchant wore a long-haired monkey cape.

Kaufe left us at the marketplace while he went to find Jacques LaMaree, our white guide and expert on pygmies. We were standing beside the car, and while Sheldon seemed unaffected by the way every native in the marketplace was staring at us, I felt frozen in place. I wanted very much to buy a basket or piece of sculpture as a souvenir, but I could not bring myself to walk into the crowd of staring, possibly unfriendly natives. I got back into the car where I felt secure and let Sheldon go into the marketplace by himself to choose something for me.

That day Sheldon had on one of his flowered shirts and all his strings of bright beads. This seemed to be the place to add to his collection, as the beads here looked most unusual. As he began to walk from display to display, he gathered a crowd of curious followers, many of whom wanted to touch him or fondle his necklaces. Soon the crowd had grown to such numbers that I could no longer see Sheldon and I became concerned for his safety.

A short time later, I heard a drum beat. The crowd spread out and formed a circle. Sheldon appeared in the center of the circle, and to my amazement, I saw that it was he who was beating the drum; a strange, hypnotic beat. Soon he began to stamp to the rhythm.

I shall never understand the full meaning of what happened next. Sheldon went into a trance and he never was able to explain the weird phenomenon, but it was as though he had cast a spell over the marketplace. Many ancient cultures believed in the magical powers of the epileptic, and I, too, am now a believer. I saw how those natives reacted to him on some intuitive level. By means of his drumbeats and dance, he somehow communicated a message to which they responded. It was a language which even he was unaware of having the knowledge of, a power he no doubt would be incapable of conveying except during those highly charged moments of *petit mal.*

What happened looked similar to a voodoo hysteria. It began with a woman swaying. More women began swaying and humming. Then men and women both were pounding out a dance around him. It soon encompassed every single individual in the marketplace. The concentration was so deep that all appeared to be in a trance just as Sheldon was. Then various people began to shudder. Women cried. A woman screamed and fell to her knees in front of him. There was a general hysteria as people became more and more affected. The sounds of moaning filled the air as everyone present seemed to be trembling with some unfathomable emotion.

Suddenly everything stopped, coming to an abrupt end! Sheldon replaced the drum as casually as if he had picked it up only that moment. He bought a string of beads as if he had spent all this time considering them. He and the people of the marketplace switched back just as if nothing had happened. The magic had vanished. So swiftly had the atmosphere changed that I became unsure of my own impressions. Fleetingly I thought that perhaps I had been overcome by the heat and imagined it all. In truth, as I was the one

154

person to witness the spell, it is only with me that the strange event lives.

Our pygmy expert, Jacques LaMaree, was a wreck of a man. Reeking of the local pombe, he was half-carried to the car by Kaufe. Once his bony frame in its baggy suit had been assisted onto the front seat of the Chevrolet, he turned to Sheldon and me in the back. As he said "Bonjour," he unleashed on us what I once heard described as dragon's breath. He spoke only French, and soon learned to direct anything he had to say to Sheldon.

Neither LaMaree's weak, skeletal appearance nor his state of intense inebriation prepared us for his aggressive personality and the way he began haggling over the price of his services—a price which was supposed to have already been fixed. But LaMaree argued that the pygmies were in the habit of turning nasty if they felt they were being underpaid. Therefore he claimed it was for our safety and not his pocket that he required the extra cash.

Although Sheldon launched into an indignant protest using his most formal and elegant French, accompanied by extravagant gestures, we were really in no position to argue with Monsieur LaMaree. There were no accommodations to be had in this part of the Congo, and even if there had been we would not have wished to stay the night. Our plan was to visit the pygmies and return to Uganda before nightfall. We could neither risk entering a pygmy village unannounced or find someone else on the spur of the moment who was qualified to make the necessary introductions. In the end we acquiesced to a sum in excess of double the original fee.

We were at the foothills and unable to proceed much further by car. Soon after we left the town, the dirt roads grew progressively steeper and more narrow, until finally Kaufe was forced to halt. By then we were near the heavily wooded mountainside which led to the pygmy village. Sheldon and I proceeded on foot with LaMaree, while Kaufe remained behind to guard the car.

Emaciated and intoxicated though he may have been, LaMaree surprisingly was a fair climber and insisted on taking the lead. At any rate it wasn't long before the heat, in addition to the climb, had all three of us gasping for breath. We became soaking wet with perspiration, as well as with the perpetual drizzle which gives the rain forest its name. Rotting leaves were slimy underfoot and the trail generally was slick and slow going. It was an altogether difficult and arduous climb through what came to feel like an endless forest on a mountain without a summit.

There were times when clouds of insects surrounded us, but fortunately they were unable to penetrate the forbidding oil Sheldon and I wore. We watched them land on LaMaree and rapidly take off again. It appeared there were no juices in his parched, wrinkled skin for even the tiniest of proboscises.

We were perhaps halfway to a clearing when LaMaree paused in his tracks, cupped a hand around puckering lips, and gave a twittering birdcall. Seconds later the same call came back from dozens of distant trees. LaMaree turned to glance over his shoulder at us. Indicating the acknowledging calls, he gave us his partially toothless grin.

The exchange of birdcalls went on for the next quarter of an hour, sometimes initiated by LaMaree and responded to by the pygmies, at other times initiated by the pygmies and answered by LaMaree. Strangely enough, the calls seemed to be spreading over an ever-widening area, yet at the same time sounded as though they were coming ever closer to us.

At first it seemed a gay, delightful method of communicating. I think I enjoyed those birdcalls until they began coming from trees not more than an arm's length away, and yet I could see no one at all. Then the calls ceased to be a chirped welcome and sounded more like a warning trill. Perhaps I was correct in my impression because LaMaree motioned for us to stop and called over his shoulder the command: "Attendez!" He then went on alone into the clearing where short black people with bulbous bellies suddenly materialized to swarm upon him.

They clutched at his skin and clothing, fidgeting and squawking like demented trolls who had captured Santa Claus. They swung on his limp, saggy jacket, turned his pocket inside out to get at the sweets he had brought them, and licked his fingers for any residue of sugar to be found there.

LaMaree then ordered them to perform. When they were in formation, singing and dancing, he motioned for Sheldon and me to join him in the clearing.

Pygmies are one of the primitive peoples who arouse the most curiosity in the western world. Sheldon and I had made this difficult trip into the Congo to observe them. Yet beyond the obvious smallness of their size, I'm not quite sure what I had expected.

I had heard conflicting reports. Some visitors had found them to be cheerful and innocent, while others had labeled them as unfriendly and dangerous. A few spoke of them as wanton slaughterers, mentally retarded, and addicted to certain intoxicating plants and berries. All agreed that they moved through the forest like veritable shadows.

I had read that they had remained at the hunter/gatherer stage of evolution, and that the forest provided all their needs. They were great hunters, and only their weapons varied from tribe to tribe: certain tribes used bows and arrows, others spears, and yet others blowpipes and darts.

Certainly there were a number of things about the pygmies which took me completely by surprise. First of all I had not expected them to be able to communicate in a perfectly respectable French. It seemed so odd to me that these totally naked creatures with their swollen stomachs, spindly legs, rotten teeth, and vile body odors should utter the poetic sounds of a Romance language. Nor had anything prepared me for those dreadfully distorted bodies which I have already partially described. I was struck in particular by the ugliness of the women's breasts, which hung to their waists on strings of flesh like long, flattened warts. Even their toy-sized children were nothing less than grotesque.

The singing-and-dancing performance they put on for us was routine and spiritless. And they all took turns in the line, holding out their hands in a gesture of begging. After the initial shock of seeing these gargoylelike people, it dawned on me that there were no men in the group. I pointed this out to Sheldon, who in turn asked LaMaree why there were no men present.

"Good Lord," Sheldon said squeezing my hand, "LaMaree tells me that the men are in the forest, and that he has brought us here at this time of day precisely to avoid them."

"I wonder why," I said.

"Well," Sheldon replied, "it seems in this tribe of Batwa, the men chew hallucinogenic berries all day long and dip the points of their arrows in poison."

A shock went through me as he said this, and I suddenly wondered what we were doing standing there. "Look, Sheldon," I said, "I have seen all of these people that I really care to see. I'm ready to leave if you are."

We told LaMaree that we had seen enough and were ready to go back to the car. Without waiting for him, we left the clearing and began our descent. But we were not to get away that easily. Immediately, the women and children abandoned their dancing and raced down the hill after us. In seconds, their clutching hands were all over us. LaMaree caught up with us and told us to ignore them and keep walking, but that was easier said than done. I wondered if he would give the chief man money at some later time, or whether the small supply of sugar and sweets he had doled out was in fact the tribe's only payment. If so, the price did not seem fair and the pygmies had a right to feel cheated.

They were all around us now begging and screaming: "Donnez-moi quelque chose!" "Sucre!" "Sucre!" "Sucre!" "Combien de cigarettes avez-vous?" "Je veux cigarette!" "Je veux Coca-Cola!" "Sucre!" "Donnez-moi bonbons!"

A chorus went up: "Bonbons!" "Bonbons!" "Bonbons!" And I remembered that I had a package of Life Savers. I took it from my shoulder bag and slowly distributed the candies, all the time continuing to inch my way down the hill. Next I gave my scarf to one and my handkerchief to another. While they studied those objects, I was able to progress forward at a faster pace.

LaMaree had advanced ahead of Sheldon and me, leaving the problem to us. Sheldon worked his way to my side and encouraged me to keep moving. He had taken a pack of playing cards from his shoulder bag and was passing them out one by one. They were brightly colored with photographs of native girls in traditional costumes and for a few minutes the attention of our pursuers was taken up in studying these pictures.

Then the car was in sight. Because it was evident that we were about to escape, the pygmies became more aggressive and began pulling at our shoulder bags, trying to peer inside. I gave one a lipstick while Sheldon gave another a pen. I found some odd sticks of chewing gum near the bottom of my bag and Sheldon discovered in his a box of melted cough drops.

We were by then at the car and Kaufe had the motor running. LaMaree was already comfortably seated in the front with his window closed and his door locked. All at once as Sheldon and I attempted to enter the car, the women became a hysterical mob. At the prospect of our leaving, they rushed us and began clawing at our clothing, shoulder bags, and hair.

We flung ourselves into the back seat and Kaufe stepped on the accelerator while the back doors were still open and with pygmies attempting to climb in. I don't believe anyone was hurt, but I can never be sure.

The car soon outdistanced them and Kaufe slowed just long enough for us to close the doors. When we turned around we saw that some of the women were still running after us, shouting and waving their arms, their long breasts flying out to their sides like flat ribbons. Suddenly, as if out of nowhere, the men joined them in their futile race to catch us. The men were stretching bowstrings and aiming at us. A hail of arrows hit the back window and fell harmlessly away.

ABOVE: The mud-gutted road that we followed into the Congo on our way to a pygmy village. BELOW: The pygmies' dance was uninspired… they were more interested in watching us! You can see the huts where they live in the background.

ABOVE: Leaving the pygmy village was as difficult as getting there, but for different reasons. They didn't want us to go, and begged for candy and anything else we had to give them. Sheldon took this photograph of me giving my scarf to a pygmy woman as we attempted to make our way back to our jeep.

BELOW: I took this photo from the back of the jeep as the pygmies chased after us.

ABOVE: Victoria Falls as viewed from the Zambian side.
BELOW: One of the many beautiful rainbows that made
the view of Victoria Falls even more spectacular.

Masked dancers in Rhodesia.

CHAPTER FIFTEEN

The evening we got back to Uganda the telephone service seemed to have ceased to function altogether, for we were unable to make any travel arrangements. We could not telephone Nairobi for a room reservation, and were unable to get through to any of Uganda's many airports to enquire about flight schedules. Early in the morning after the Congo trip, we decided to drive to Entebbe and take our chances. Consequently, we missed the direct flight to Nairobi by fifteen minutes and were obliged to get on the milk run, which made five prior stops.

It was almost noon when we disembarked and I suggested we go directly to the New Stanley. With any luck we might find a room there. We wanted to deposit our luggage, have some small refreshment, and go to the hospital to see Cathy and Susan.

While Sheldon was paying the taxi, I walked onto the veranda to briefly look around. Suddenly I let out a cry of joy. Seated at a center table was Bert, with Cathy on one side of him and Susan on the other! Cathy had a bit of discoloration under one eye and Susan's legs had a tender, pink look, but other than that, they both appeared to be exceedingly well.

"I can't believe it!" I gasped running up to them. "Sheldon and I were about to go to the hospital to visit you! When were you released?"

"This morning," Bert said. "Isn't it great! They took off Susan's bandages an hour ago!"

"They wanted me to leave yesterday," Cathy said, tossing her blond hair to cover the eye where the skin was still bruised. "But Susan and I were sharing a room and I didn't want to check out and leave her there alone."

Susan broke out laughing. "You were afraid if you left me alone," she softly pinched Cathy's arm and continued, "they would cut off my legs and I wouldn't know the difference."

Cathy pouted and playfully tapped Susan on the nose.

"But that's amazing," I said to Bert. "They were in the hospital less than a week."

"Today is the seventh day since they entered the hospital," Bert said. "The eighth since the accident . . ."

Cathy interrupted him, "And guess what? You're in for another surprise. Mac flew in from Tsavo for the day. And he brought his wife with him."

"Oh, that's wonderful! Sally, too? Where is she?"

Susan pointed down the street. "She's gone shopping. Mac is in the lobby making some phone calls."

It turned out to be Sally MacKenna's birthday, and a day to be remembered. A day when we all were together with so many things to celebrate and be grateful for. I recall that afternoon as one of the most pleasant of the trip.

Sally MacKenna's proper birthday celebration was to be held at

Tsavo that evening, but Mac had insisted that she take the day off from her responsibilities so that he could fly her to Nairobi for some shopping and a special lunch. Sally was partial to the curry at the Norfolk Hotel and Mac invited us all to join them.

Sheldon and I were able to check into the New Stanley because we were willing to accept a suite for one night. It was actually most convenient on that particular day to have a sitting room and an extra bathroom. We were able to invite our friends to share the accommodations for the purpose of preparing for the special luncheon.

The men found no need to change clothes, but Cathy and I put on dresses, and I lent Susan a lacy blouse to wear for the occasion. Sally MacKenna was such a tall, buxom woman that she more easily found separates in her size. She had bought an orange organdy blouse to match an orange-brown skirt. I remembered Sally's longing for the flowers of civilization and the precious little cyclamen she had so generously presented to me at our last meeting. When I saw that she had added to her new outfit a hat of pale orange straw covered in artificial daisies of brown, orange, yellow, and white, I smiled at her with unconcealed affection.

The Norfolk Hotel was on a distant hill removed from the hubbub of Nairobi's traffic. Its old-fashioned dining room was long and wide, with enough tables to accommodate the entire permanent community and still have space for visitors, tourists and safari groups. Large fans whirred overhead, and walls of screened windows connected with the screened porches where you took your cocktail before the meal and relaxed afterwards over a coffee and brandy. It had an old-world quiet and charm, the type of atmosphere in which Sally MacKenna felt most at home. We were there on one of the two days of the week when they offered a sumptuous buffet of curries along with all the trimmings.

One hardly noticed the extreme heat of the day while seated on one of the porches of the Norfolk, with its endless screened windows and large ceiling fans. There on the hill, not far from the Nairobi Museum which housed Dr. Leakey's finds, a slight breeze was circulating and the chintz cushions of the white wicker furniture felt smoothly fresh and cool to the touch. We all had chosen the extra-hot curries from the buffet table and that, too, had produced a lowering of the external body temperature. At the end of the meal, rather than hurrying away to take the customary siesta, we ordered a strong Turkish coffee and spent the afternoon on the porch enjoying one another's company.

Mac had been listening intently to our reports of the conditions we had found in Uganda and the Congo. He was deeply concerned about the changing face of Africa. Politically, many of the black African countries were being infiltrated by foreign extremists who were backing local thugs. Rumors, although difficult to confirm, were getting back to Kenya about every type of injustice being perpetrated—from secret imprisonment to mass murder.

Uganda was considered an unsafe country, as was the Congo, but perhaps even more so was Zambia, where we were next heading.

"You say this Ugandan, Richard Mbowa, warned you to stay out of Zambia?" Mac asked.

I said, "Yes, he felt quite strongly about it."

Sheldon hurriedly put in, "We want to see the Victoria Falls from the Zambian side. We'll only be there for a few days and we won't venture anywhere beyond the popular tourist spots."

Mac shook his head of reddish-brown hair, scratched his beard, and looked at us with consternation.

It was Sally who said, "Why not see the falls from the Rhodesian side? You'll still get a good view, and Rhodesia is a safe country."

"She's right," Mac said. "Rhodesia has just law and police protection. You ought to sacrifice a little of the view of the falls for the sake of your own safety."

"And," Sally added, "when you get on the bridge near the

falls . . . you know, Mac, the bridge that links Zambia and Rhodesia . . ."

"The Zambezi Bridge," Mac interjected.

"Yes. Well, there are often snipers nearby. So stay well away from the Zambian end of the bridge."

In the end we did not take the advice of Richard Mbowa or the MacKennas, and Sheldon and I would deeply regret it. Warnings so often are futile. One always feels that tragedy is something which strikes other people and never oneself. At the time we were consumed by a desire to see the Victoria Falls from the best possible vantage point, and that was at Livingstone in Zambia. Bert, Cathy, and Susan also chose to dismiss the dangers. Fired by our enthusiasm, they were going to set out in the camper that evening and join us in Livingstone in two days' time.

For Sheldon and me it meant flying to the capital, Lusaka, and then driving the two hundred miles to the falls. Once Sally and Mac were on their way back to Tsavo, we hurried to the New Stanley to consult the travel agency in the lobby. As it happened, even getting into Zambia was not a simple matter. The travel agent sent a messenger to Government House to have visas stamped in our passports while Sheldon and I rushed to the nearest bank. We were obliged to fly Zambian Airways, and they only accepted payment in cash and in their own currency: the kwacha.

It was rather miraculous how we accomplished everything for the next morning's journey in what remained of the afternoon. Aside from the complex travel arrangements, new luggage was a priority since our cases had been demolished by the hyenas. The bazaars stayed open late and had a large selection of goods. We were able to find some sturdy cases which were nonetheless attractive, and I was able to make my long overdue purchase of a camera so that I might begin taking photographs in earnest. Since, however, I am a hopeless amateur, I decided to stay with a camera which does almost everything automatically.

The one detail which Sheldon and I overlooked in our rush was the changing of money. It had been nearly the close of banking hours. We needed such a large amount of kwacha for the air tickets that we had cashed only the exact amount of travelers checks. In any case, the Zambian government permitted a tourist to bring in only ten kwacha, equivalent to fourteen dollars, which would not have gone very far.

Upon arriving in a new country one is always able to change money at the airport bank, and therefore it had not occurred to us to purchase the extra kwacha for our wallets. Even if we had, I doubt seriously that we would have foreseen a need to change a one-kwacha note into one hundred ngwees. But, oh my, when we arrived in Lusaka, what we would have not given for just one ngwee apiece!

When we landed at Lusaka Airport, we were astonished to see that the terminal building was nothing more than an open shed. It had one deserted ticket counter and a solitary Bantu working as a porter. It was difficult to believe that this was what had become of the principal airport which served the capital. There were no customs officials to check our suitcases or our newly acquired visas. At first we weren't concerned at the absence of a bank because we had travelers checks and credit cards, as well as pounds sterling, French francs, and U.S. dollars.

The passengers who had been on the plane with us were a tour group on a packaged holiday and were whisked away in a specially chartered bus. Sheldon and I sat on an outside bench for a time waiting for a taxi, but none appeared. We approached the sole porter and asked him if there were some way of calling a cab.

He said, "No taxis come. Bus come later."

"What about a car hire?" Sheldon asked him.

"One garage. Down road . . . there," he said, pointing down the long, straight tarmac road where there were absolutely no structures in sight.

I asked him how far away the garage was but he was unable to say and just kept repeating: "Down road . . . there." Sheldon paid him to guard our luggage and we set out on foot down the deserted road. By then it was late morning, hot and humid, and the most uncomfortable part of the day. Every step of the walk seemed a great effort.

Forty-five minutes later we saw a garage in the distance but there didn't seem to be any activity. We began to worry that perhaps the owners were napping.

We found a young Bantu asleep in a chair, in a shady spot at the side of the building. He told us that he had a car to rent and showed us a dilapidated Mini. Sheldon tried it first to make sure it was in running condition. The young man had the official three-copy rental paper, but was at a loss as to how to fill it in. So while Sheldon read out the mileage, the amount of gasoline, the license number, and so on, I filled in the form. When I reached the space which read *Price,* I said it aloud and looked up at the young man for his reply.

"Four thousand," he said.

"Four thousand what?" Sheldon asked.

"Four thousand dollars," he replied.

"No, you don't understand," I said trying not to lose my temper. "We do not wish to buy the car."

"These papers," Sheldon explained, speaking with slow exaggerated enunciation, "are hire . . . rental hire forms. We wish . . . to rent . . . the car . . . for . . . one week."

"Four thousand dollars of the United States," the young man said easily, for he was unperturbed.

"The rental price cannot be four thousand dollars a week," Sheldon said trying to control his voice. "What is . . . rental?"

The boy smiled in comprehension. "Rental is twenty-five dollars each day."

"Well, that's more like it," Sheldon said, patting him on the back.

The boy again smiled and added, "And four thousand dollars."

Sheldon and I were speechless for a time. The boy asked to see the form. Then pointing to the space which read *Rental,* he told us, "Rental is twenty-five dollars each day, United States." Then pointing to the space which read *Security Deposit,* he said, "This is four thousand dollars."

"Four thousand dollars as a deposit!" Sheldon screamed. "Let me see that form."

The young man smiled by way of encouraging us and added brightly, "You bring back car . . . I give you four thousand dollars United States."

When we looked as if we still doubted his word he said flatly, "It is law of Zambia . . . not me."

Thoroughly discouraged, we walked back to the airport where we waited perhaps another hour without seeing activity of any kind. There was not a soul present but us. Even the porter had disappeared, along with our luggage.

Around three o'clock a large bus pulled in and without a word to each other, Sheldon and I rose in unison and swiftly walked toward it. Just as we arrived, the front doors of the bus opened with that puffing hydraulic sound. An enormous black in a bus driver's uniform stepped out and the doors immediately closed behind him. Ignoring us, he strode by and directly toward the toilet. We followed closely behind, calling out to him. He nodded his head in the affirmative to our most important questions: the bus was going to Livingstone and it was going this afternoon. What we didn't know was at what hour. When the driver returned to the bus, we did not again confront him, but we sat and watched closely in case he made a move to drive off.

At four o'clock we heard the noise of a plane coming in for a landing. From around the corner of the terminal building we saw a trolley with our luggage on it being pushed by the returning porter.

Only six passengers arrived. All of us and the luggage were

quickly dispatched onto the bus, and the driver closed the doors. Then the driver levered himself out of his seat and plodded down the aisle to collect our fares. Sheldon and I were seated nearest to the driver's seat. When he loomed over us and said: "One ngwee," we thought perhaps it was Zambian for "good evening."

Then he said again, "One ngwee," and this time it sounded almost like a threat.

The woman across the aisle from us said, "It's the Zambian currency. There are one hundred ngwees to one kwacha."

"Can that be correct?" I asked. "At the exchange rate we got yesterday of one-point-four, that would make a ngwee worth less than two pennies."

"That's right . . . by my exchange chart," she said, handing it to us. "You see there . . . one ngwee is worth one and one fourth cents."

The driver had worked his way to the back and had accosted the five other passengers, four of whom had the required single ngwee. The remaining passenger, a man with a German accent, had a single kwacha note but the driver had not enough change.

The woman across the aisle from us had emptied the contents of her purse into her lap. She looked up at the driver on his return and said nervously, "Just a minute, I probably have one somewhere."

Sheldon said, "I know we don't have any Zambian money." Then he held up in a fan: a dollar, a pound, and a franc. "Take your pick," he said. "No change necessary."

"One ngwee," the driver said, glaring at us.

Sheldon turned to the man in the back with the kwacha note and asked him, "May I buy that from you and pay everyone's fare?"

"I would be happy to do that myself," the man said in the deep guttural tones of his German accent, "but the driver insists on one ngwee from each of us. He doesn't have change and I don't believe he understands any language other than his own."

Someone reasoned that the porter was bound to have change.

The German motioned for the driver to open the doors; he got out and went in search of the porter.

The woman across from us found a ngwee in the lining of her purse and began giggling in relief.

The driver took a framed notice from the rack above our heads and showed it to us. It read: GOVERNMENT REGULATIONS REQUIRE EACH PASSENGER TO PRESENT DRIVER WITH ONE NGWEE COIN.

The man with the kwacha note came back to say that the porter apparently had gone home for the day. We pleaded with the driver to accept some other currency, or the kwacha note, or take us to a place where we could get change. But the mammoth driver was unmoved in his stance for one ngwee each.

"What are we going to do, darling?" I whispered.

"Nothing. We are not leaving this bus under any circumstances. He simply has to take us to Livingstone. I'm not going to have us sitting up all night in the middle of nowhere in an open terminal building."

But the driver was about to throw us off the bus physically and so we got off peacefully. As he put our luggage on the ground, I held up my gold wristwatch and offered it to him. But he shook his head and said probably the only words in English he knew: "One ngwee."

"At least the man was honest," I said as the bus pulled away. Then tears which I'd had difficulty holding back welled up in my eyes.

"He's a bloody stupid black monkey," said the German with the kwacha note.

"You're South African?" Sheldon said.

"That is correct. My name is Hans Rohan," he said extending his hand.

Sheldon was about to introduce us, but I interrupted belligerently by saying, "We do not believe in apartheid!" Then looking around me at our isolation, I burst into uncontrollable tears.

Sheldon put his arm around me saying, "Don't cry, my darling, we'll find some way out of this mess."

Hans hit the palm of one hand with the fist of the other and swore under his breath. Then he puffed heavily and addressed himself to us: "So you do not believe in apartheid? Everybody knows the blacks are mentally inferior. But we admit it openly. We don't trust them but we don't mistreat them. We just refuse to give them the rope to hang us with as they are doing to themselves as well as the whites in every country where they have been given independence. Compare Ian Smith's Southern Rhodesia with this mess of a country which used to be Northern Rhodesia . . . before the blacks divided it by getting the one-monkey one-vote law passed."

"Look," Sheldon said sharply, "I could discuss this with you forcefully by reminding you of all the many areas where the black people have been successful. But right now we are stuck in the middle of nowhere and it will be getting dark soon. Shouldn't we discuss our next move?"

I thought I had calmed down but I repeated to Hans, "We don't believe in apartheid," and immediately burst into tears again at the thought of all the injustice in the world; our being put off the bus, as well as apartheid.

"You don't believe in apartheid," Hans rasped with a short, bitter laugh. "Stay in this part of Rhodesia . . . which the monkeys now call Zambia . . . for some days and you will be just as firm a believer as I am."

"Are you as good at getting us out of this mess as you are at segregation?" I snapped at Hans.

"Of course, a car passes now and then," he said smugly. "We simply hitchhike a ride."

"Oh, terrific idea," I retorted. "We simply get into a car of bandits and let them rob and murder us."

"Open that bag of mine, little missus," he said, "and you will see why we have no need to fear anyone."

I unzipped the top of his golf-club bag and quickly closed it again. I had seen a light rifle and a heavy rifle and something that might have been a machine gun. "Oh, my God! Are you some kind of terrorist?"

Roaring with laughter, he said, "I am a professional big-game hunter with a license to carry guns."

Then Hans opened his jacket and showed us his shoulder holster and gun. "But I also intend to protect myself while I am in this barbaric country . . . where, by the way, the blacks are controlled by the Chinese Communists. Kaunda's government is merely their puppet."

I must still have appeared terrified, because he added in a softer tone, "Would I have let myself be thrown off a bus if I were a terrorist? Of course not. I did not use my guns to hijack that bus."

We heard a car engine in the distance. It sounded to be coming very fast and from the wrong direction to give us a ride to Livingstone. When it was nearly on top of us it skidded to a stop. By the markings on the car and the navy-and-white uniforms the two black men wore, we assumed they were some branch of the police.

They spoke no language we could comprehend and everything was communicated in signs. They checked our passports and other documents. From the hotel chits they knew we three were going to Livingstone, but not to the same lodgings. Sheldon and I were booked at the Grand Central Hotel, literally a few yards from the falls, and Hans was staying at the Zambezi Gorge Hunters' Lodge, which was close to the gorge.

I was praying that they wouldn't ask us to open our luggage, discover Hans's arsenal of weapons, and throw us in prison. But they tossed our cases, unopened, into the trunk of the car. They then drove us into Livingstone at an unrelieved ninety miles an hour. I knew that if any big game happened to cross the road, this would be our last ride!

They slowed down just before reaching Livingstone town center and a few minutes later dropped us off at the bus station. Sheldon and I had had enough of buses for one day and we hailed a taxi. We had also had quite enough of Hans and did not offer to share our taxi with him.

CHAPTER SIXTEEN

We heard a thundering as our taxi approached the falls. It was after dark, but appointed spotlights revealed huge, billowing clouds, as though gigantic fires were producing a pure white smoke. The natives called them Musi-o-Tunya: The Smoke That Thunders. In 1855, Dr. Livingstone was the first white man to behold this natural wonder and he had honored his monarch by naming it Victoria.

The hotel could not have been more perfectly designed or situated. In deference to the falls, every room had sliding doors which opened onto a patio. These extended to a lawn from which one overlooked a broad chasm, the other side of which was the widest expanse of falling water in all the world.

The mist enveloped us the moment we stepped outside our sliding doors, the thundering sound vibrated through us, and the first sight of the Victoria Falls took our breath away. As we walked toward this awe-inspiring spectacle, we became giddy as well, because there were no guard railings. The lawn ended in a sheer drop where thousands of tons of water smashed against the rocks below and bounced back to form great frothy clouds.

Sheldon and I stood at the edge clinging to one another, permitting the wet updraft to rush at us from the bottom of the gorge, thrilling to the danger of knowing that one tiny step forward could plunge us headlong into the abyss.

To our right some tourists with relatively useless umbrellas were negotiating the Knife Edge Bridge. It was constructed between two mountain tops and faced the curtain of falling water. We waited until they had reentered their rooms. Then we left the edge of our lawn in favor of the delicious illusion of risk embodied on that narrow bridge. Sheldon ran across it without looking down and I followed. The water soaked us through and felt icy cold, but the night was mild and we didn't care about our clothing getting wet after the sweat of the day. We became progressively more courageous about the height, so that eventually we were able to stop midway and study the dynamic churning of the waters below us.

It was quite late by the time we had unpacked, showered, and dressed for dinner. But we were so totally enchanted by those magnificent falls that we rushed through dinner and afterwards sat out on our patio with the mist covering us, watching the spotlights playing through the voluminous cascading waters. When we made love, we stretched out on the bathroom rug, taking off our damp clothes but not bothering to dry ourselves.

The next time we looked through the sliding doors no one seemed to be about, so we put on our bathing suits and ran out to romp by the falls. We screamed and raced over the narrow bridge as the freezing cold spray lashed us with millions of sparkling pellets.

Living beside the falls was romantic and stirring almost beyond compare. After making love yet again and sleeping only a brief time, we awoke as the sun was beginning to rise.

We struggled into our still-wet swimsuits and hurried out onto the bridge to greet the morning. The frosty shower soon washed the sleep from our eyes. With the sun fully up, there came the rainbows—arches of color in every direction one looked. Shifting prisms of watery glory moved and danced with each blink of the eye. It was little wonder that this spot had become one of the most talked-about sights in all of Africa. And the temptation of being this close to the falls, which was only possible here on the Zambian side, was understandably irresistible. Nevertheless, the strict, petty and annoying government regulations along with the rumors of danger were enough to keep all but a handful of tourists away.

After breakfast we walked the two miles to the tourist office in the town center. We hoped to rent a car so that we might be able to see something of the surrounding countryside. The black girl behind the counter with dozens of tiny braids in her hair told us that a government regulation did, indeed, require a security deposit of four thousand dollars. However, for just ten additional dollars per day on top of the rental fee, we could hire a chauffeur-driven car and bypass the deposit. It sounded like a good deal, and we hired a chauffeur-driven car for that day and possibly the next, or at least until Bert arrived with his camper.

Our driver was a member of the Bemba-speaking peoples, a very pleasant, jolly fellow, and when he told us his name was Singazonga, we could not resist calling him as his name sounded to us: Sing-a-song-a. He was able to communicate in English, or at least he seemed to understand what we were saying, even if he had difficulty at times in finding the English words in which to express himself. Sheldon and I wanted to take a drive first to the shores of the Zambezi nearest the drop, so that we might see the top of the falls.

Singazonga asked us please to be careful on the banks of the river as dangerous creatures like crocodiles and poisonous snakes lurked there. He told us that in Zambia there were few safety measures. You did everything at your own risk. Because anyone might go anywhere he pleased on foot, Zambia was famous for the walking safari. He told us all of this with an expression of extreme distaste and, indeed, we were never to witness the sensible Singazonga walk more than a few feet from the safety of the car.

In Central Africa one experiences a strong sense of isolation. Certainly there are fewer outside influences than in East Africa, where one is constantly aware of being at the crossroads of both Eastern and Western cultures. On the banks of the Zambezi River, for miles in all directions, it must be as it was when Dr. Livingstone first saw it. The bulging baobabs are ancient, and there are species of trees and plants which have never deviated from their original form.

We carefully picked our way from the road to the river bank, all the while swinging a stick through the grass before taking a step ahead. We were close to the falls, but the Zambezi was not raging to the precipice as we had expected. It was flowing placidly around sandbars and patches of reeds. Neither were there rapids preceding the plunge, only flat, grayish water which suddenly, without warning, dropped over the edge.

In those calm waters above the falls, gray camouflaged forms were gliding, barely making a ripple. Near us was a sign which said it all: SWIMMING IS SUICIDAL!

Yet again, I scanned the river bank on either side of us but nothing was moving. A band of white-throated grivet monkeys were swinging in the treetops. As they tore through the branches above us, a vine fell. It grazed my shoulder and I nearly fainted with fright, thinking it was a snake.

The grivets clambered to the ground about twenty yards from us and went to the river's edge. As I watched the monkeys, I saw nothing in the waters where they bent to drink. Yet, in the next instant, enormous jaws came from the depths to the surface and clamped onto the body of one of them. There were terrible shrieks from the others. Powerful jaws began to twist. As the crocodile cannot chew, it spins its prey until a piece breaks off. The grivets had backed out of danger, but stayed to scream and scold, jumping up and down in protest. The victim did not break in half and the crocodile unwound, dropping it. It looked as if the crocodile were paying heed to the anger of the band of monkeys, but in fact a crocodile will drown if it continues to twist in that fashion. So if a piece of meat does not come away easily, he must abandon the prey. That did the grivet little good. It was already quite dead and floating slowly toward the falls.

For a time we traced the Zambezi upstream on foot, but on seeing that the landscape ahead remained more or less unchanged, we decided to go back to the road and find the car. Singazonga next drove us until we reached the leafy riverside drive outside of Livingstone where the view was less predictable. Although we were in the tropics the heat was not oppressive, as this part of the country lies on a high plateau. It is a plateau rising anywhere from three to seven thousand feet above sea level, and extending all the way from South Africa to the Sahara Desert in the north.

The vegetation was more abundant now, and wooded hillsides dotted the horizon. We saw in the thicket some sable antelopes with their splendid backward-curving horns, and asked Singazonga to stop the car so that we might photograph them. At the same time, we noticed that there was a van parked at the roadside close to where we wanted to pull over.

"Let's get out here, near that van," Sheldon said. "If we go on foot we can get close enough for some good shots, even though we don't have telephoto lenses."

"I wouldn't go there, Mister Sir," Singazonga said. "Buffalo and rhino are in those hills . . . have special paths through there to the river."

"We will be careful, Singazonga," Sheldon told him.

"Also men hunting now . . . see?" Singazonga said pointing to the van. It was painted in black-and-white zebra stripes and the lettering on the side read ZAMBEZI GORGE HUNTING LODGE.

"Isn't that where the South African is staying?" I asked.

"Hans Rohan, yes, it is," Sheldon said. "Good Lord, I hope we don't stumble into that dreadful boor!"

"There are so few tourists about, he could easily be the only hunter at the lodge."

"Got your camera loaded, darling?" Sheldon asked.

"I'm ready to take a masterpiece or two," I said. "Let me know if you see any galagos."

Sheldon looked puzzled. "See any what?"

"Ha, got you there!" I laughed. "Bush babies."

We had only gone a short distance into the thicket when we turned back toward the road to discover we had already lost sight of the car. In front of us were thick trees, but through them we got glimpses of the river sparkling in the sunlight. The hills which Singazonga had spoken of were to our right, and that was where the sable antelope were heading. The prevailing wind was coming off the hills, so we were able to follow the sables without their picking up our scent. We put one foot down silently before lifting the other. Although we were hunting with cameras rather than guns, the sport of stalking the animals was in no way diminished.

We followed close to the river bank where the Zambezi was hidden behind a wall of reeds. The heavily leafed branches of trees hung over to touch the reed wall, and we walked underneath in the cool shaded avenue. There were intriguing sounds of flutterings and scurryings and swooshings. At one moment there was a break in the reed wall and there, swimming in the water in front of us, was a family of creamy-coated otters. Dragonflies of the most spectacular color hovered above the surface, and bullfrogs half hidden by reeds were nonetheless drawing attention to themselves by making croaking noises. For the moment we had lost sight of the sable antelope, but I pointed to the high ridge of jutting hillside in the distance where two rhinos stood surveying the lay of the land.

I don't think we had gone much further before we became enclosed in a tunnel of thickets, reeds, and hanging branches. Here there was the strong musky smells of animals. The slough of reeds and mud beneath our feet looked to be a well-traveled path. All at once I was gripped by fear and wanted desperately to be out in the open. What would happen to us if some big bull, a buffalo or rhino, came barging along that tunnel?

Sheldon showed little regard for his own well-being. I think it was because he was so anxious to live every minute to its fullest. Certainly, quite early in our relationship, I had realized that he was almost a complete fatalist. I remembered how, when we were stranded on the island, he could have easily resigned himself to dying. He didn't seem to take his own life seriously, somehow. Others' lives, yes, but not his own.

What should I do? Persuade him to turn back? What happened if a rhino charged and we were too far inside this tunnel to retreat to safety? Even after realizing a danger, how many people have died simply because they reacted too slowly? Would that happen to us? Would I be trampled to death thinking "What a fool I was to have delayed!" Of course, if I spoke the sound would lose us the antelope.

Then the river made a bend to the right and we were away from the trees, in the open, but following the same game trail through tall grass. The reeds at the bank were so thick we could not see two feet into them. Now, the wind changed and blew hard from behind us. On a hilly slope far in the distance, we caught sight of the sables' antlers. They turned and looked directly at us. The animals began to run.

"We can't catch up with them now," I said tugging at Sheldon's sleeve. "Why don't we turn back?"

We had had no hint that we, too, were being followed, even as we were following the sables. We were startled to hear a human voice coming from close behind us: "They heard you chattering . . . that is why they are running away," said the South African. It was Hans Rohan with a tracker. The tracker eased ahead of us and toward some dung. He stooped close over it. Hans also passed us to get to the dung.

He bent down looking at it and said, "There is blood in his droppings. I got that rhino with a gut shot."

I hate it when a man tries to make me feel my actions are silly and ill-considered because I'm a female. I walked up to Hans and said in a low, but defiant voice, "I was not chattering. I know to be quiet. I spoke only after the antelope took off."

Hans replied, "Only kidding, little missus." But he said it coldly and without looking at me. "The fact is they winded us . . . so they bolted." Then he turned sharply and commanded me, "Now! Be silent!"

"Don't worry, we'll be leaving you!" I said, but in a voice that came out too high-pitched with emotion.

Then Hans gazed at me with an air of maddening superiority, tinged with a hint of sexual leering. "For your own protection, you will stay right behind me," he said smugly, and then he turned his back on me yet again.

I believe I was ready to fly into a rage but Sheldon came up behind me and gripped me by the shoulders. He leaned in close and whispered to me, "Darling, we've got no choice . . . not with a wounded rhino nearby. We will have to stay with them . . . either until they kill it or give up the search and escort us back to the road."

So I was forced to swallow my pride and stay behind the boor —the boring, boorish Boer!—whom I hated. I was forced to accept his protection and allow him to flaunt his machismo. I found his power, strength, and confidence made me feel feminine, giddy, and sexually tingly . . . and then I despised myself for feeling that way.

The danger, too, was a forceful stimulant. All my nerve endings seemed to be on the surface of my skin. A flock of geese flew overhead, and I shuddered involuntarily at the sudden rush of wings.

We proceeded through sharp grasses higher than our heads; first the tracker, then Hans, followed by me and then Sheldon. Sharp blades of the grass nicked the exposed skin on our arms. The sun was fierce and the band on my canvas hat no longer kept the sweat from running into my eyes. As we began a gradual climb the breeze blew the grass in waves. White fingers of clouds sped across the sky. I wanted water because my mouth was painfully dry and the back of my throat had turned to cotton wool. But I preferred to die of thirst rather than ask Hans for a drink from his canteen. I placed my feet in the tracks he made, and followed his broad shoulders and the barrel of his gun, which rested over the left one.

We crossed an overgrown gully and began climbing a steep, grassy ridge. Then we stopped. The tracker pointed up to a thicket of thorn trees at the edge of a forest. There was the rhino, his horn showing clearly and his mud-covered coat looking almost red in the sun. He sniffed the air briefly before moving with a short-legged, weary pace into the darkness of the trees.

The tracker went on alone now. Hans turned and motioned for us to sit in the shade and rest. He unfastened the strap and handed the canteen first to me. It took all my willpower to sip slowly . . . and only three short sips . . . before I pushed it abruptly in front of myself at arms' length, as though at that distance I could no longer be tempted to take more. I didn't look at Hans but somehow I knew he was grinning. From the corner of my eye I saw him hand the canteen to Sheldon. It was only when Hans took the canteen and turned away from us that I succumbed to the heat, slumping against the tree and using my neck scarf to dry my face.

Our rest period was all too brief. Soon the tracker was back and we were climbing but making a wide circle around the area where the rhino had entered the densest part of the forest. It was much too thick in there for them to get a clear view for a shot, so we were going to attempt to find the wounded rhino when he came out the other side.

We stopped to listen. Tick birds were nearby. There were strawy piles of elephant dung and a trail of their uprooted trees, but no elephants. Suddenly things happened in split-second flashes, yet with the seeming slow-motion quality of a dream. We saw the rhino's blood-clotted dung . . . then a line of tiny blood droplets . . . his tracks . . . in fact, all the fresh rhino signs . . . but no rhino. His arrival was heralded by a single shooshing snort. He charged, head down, horn straight at us, short legs thundering, and with the speed of a locomotive.

I froze in place with an image of him skewering us one after the other on his horn in a human kabob. Both Hans and the tracker had their rifles raised . . . but for some reason they did not fire. The rhino was on top of us and we all were about to breathe our last. Only then did I hear the tiny whunking sound of a bullet. Such a small, vulgar, mean way to put out the life of such a noble, prehistoric creature. A creature which belonged to that great primeval landscape.

Hans had waited with nerves of steel until the very last second and then had put the barrel straight into the jugular. The great beast crashed to its knees at his feet, an arcing stream of blood cascading over the hunter: the rhino paying final homage to his destroyer.

I never saw the fountain of blood dwindle. I turned hot and cold and nauseous and then lost consciousness with that image of spewing blood still before me.

Next I remembered choking on fire and gasping for breath. Sheldon was holding my head and giving me brandy from Hans's flask. I must only have been out momentarily, because Hans and the tracker were just beginning to cut away the flesh in order to get at the rhino's horn. Sheldon and I left the scene without a word to them and found our own way out of the maze and back to the car.

Once we were at the hotel, I fell into bed and thought of possibly sleeping straight through the night. An hour later the phone rang, and it was Bert. He, Cathy, and Susan had just arrived in Livingstone. They had seen a sign advertising a Sundowner Cruise on a river boat up the Zambezi above the falls. It sounded lovely and the thought revived my spirits. Sheldon and I hurriedly showered and dressed.

CHAPTER SEVENTEEN

Our riverboat was a charming, old-fashioned stern-wheeler and it burnt as fuel a freshly scented cyprus. We heard the rippling sounds of the river around us as well as the distant crash of the falls. Within the everpresent mist, we witnessed rainbows newly born of a fiery setting sun. Hippos and crocodiles and all manner of river life glided by us as though appearing for our cocktail-hour entertainment. Indeed, arranging a cruise above the falls at sunset was a truly inspirational idea.

Cathy, Susan, and I were content to sit by ourselves at a table overlooking the hypnotic waters, sipping our white wine and making no attempt to mingle with the other guests.

Earlier at the hotel, Sheldon had spoken to a group of school teachers. Now they were attempting to isolate him as if he were the last man alive. They were crowded around him, and he was talking animatedly about his travels, probably thinking that was what the ladies were attracted by. Sheldon was either unaware of his youthful good looks, or took them so much for granted that he had forgotten just how appealing he was to women. I looked the ladies over and as none of them seemed to present any particular threat, I could enjoy the attention they were lavishing on my lover.

Bert had fallen in with a group of hunters from the game lodge, some of whom, even at cocktail hour, carried a gun. Hans was among them, and unfortunately Bert had struck up a friendship with him. I distrusted the South African's motives. I had the feeling that he was courting Bert in order to get closer to our group, or perhaps just to me.

Bert more or less accepted an invitation for all of us to have dinner at the lodge with Hans and his friends. It seemed somehow awkward for Sheldon and me to refuse, so we went along with the arrangement.

The lodge was spotlessly clean, with an atmosphere of severity and starkness which I tend to think of as Germanic. When, along with the half-dozen varieties of game, we were served sauerkraut and German-style potato salad, I thought my assumption must be correct.

Throughout the evening Hans was a gentleman, playing the gracious host. He and the others were making an effort to be polite to the ladies, while being careful not to show any untoward attention to us. Susan and Cathy seemed to be having a wonderful time, as did Bert, so Sheldon and I simply winked at one another.

After dinner, Hans suggested that we see the Makishi pole dancing. The Maramba Cultural Center which featured traditional dancing was in Livingstone, but Hans dismissed it as being staged for tourists. He coaxed us to go over the border to a private club in Rhodesia, which was just the other side of the Zambezi Bridge and not much further away than Livingstone.

We traveled in the game lodge's black-and-white van along with two other cars belonging to the hunters. I remembered Sally telling us not to go on that bridge because of the sniper fire, but it was a quiet night and we crossed without incident. However, once on the Rhodesian side of the bridge, one of the border guards recognized me from my films and made a point of warning me. He told me it was foolish to have left possessions in a hotel room in Zambia. According to him, Zambian border guards gave to thieves the room numbers of tourists going into Rhodesia. While they were away, their rooms were sacked. He left me with another strong warning: "Get out of that country as quickly as possible!" Then with a smile he added, "Come over to our side. We will protect you."

At the nightclub, when I had the opportunity to be alone with Cathy in the ladies room, I told her what the guard had said. We agreed between us to persuade Bert and Sheldon to move our location to the Rhodesian side after the morning's viewing of the falls.

Cathy wasted no time in talking to Bert and Susan about transferring across the border and they both agreed without an argument. I had neglected to express my feelings about Hans Rohan to Cathy, and she discussed the move in front of him. To my great dismay, Hans asked if he too might hitch a ride in Bert's camper, as he planned to leave Zambia tomorrow. At that stage, there seemed to be no way I could intervene, so it was decided that the six of us would move out of Zambia in Bert's camper at noon the next day.

In the morning Bert, Cathy, and Susan came to our hotel, where one had the best view of the falls. Hans was due to join us as well, but I didn't want to play hostess to him. So while Sheldon entertained our guests, I had Singazonga drive me to the tourist office so that I could cancel our car and settle the bill. I was sorry to say good-bye to Singazonga, but we no longer needed a car now that

Bert could provide us with transportation, and we were unlikely to return to Zambia.

After the mileage check, Singazonga drove away and I planned to take a taxi back to the hotel. Inside the tourist office I had a long wait while they calculated the bill, so I flicked through a magazine. At first there had been two young girls, both with those masses of tiny braids in their hair. They had been studying my rental contract as though it were an examination in higher calculus. Now I glanced up to see that they had been replaced by a black man in an incongruous brown Maoist uniform. He seemed to be making out an entirely new contract for me. I thought about questioning him, but decided it might be better to have patience and wait until he had finished, so I went back to my magazine. It was then that some heavy footsteps drew my attention. Three Chinese soldiers with machine guns had entered and stood at attention behind the counter.

At first I was only puzzled. It seemed odd to see Chinese soldiers. And why have machine guns in a tourist office?

The African in the Maoist suit gestured for me to come to the counter. I remembered thinking how unnecessarily rude he was. Instead of asking me, he almost accused me when he said, "With what means do you intend to pay?"

I took out my folder of credit cards but he put his hand over it and brusquely slammed it to the counter. "No credit cards," he said sharply. The three soldiers with machine guns had not moved, but they were glaring at me. It was then that I became frightened. Oh God, was this really happening to me? In bright daylight in a tourist office?

The bill should have been thirty-five dollars plus mileage. I had expected that they might charge me for today as well, and also that they might not wish to accept credit cards, so I had brought along a hundred dollars in cash. The man pushed in front of me a statement for six hundred dollars!

I got out my traveler's checks. I had seven hundred dollars left. When he saw me counting them, he added two hundred dollars in tax to my bill and changed the total to eight hundred dollars. He swept up my hundred dollars in cash. Then he shoved a pen in my hand and said, "Sign!" I was acutely aware of the soldiers with their machine guns and I had no intention of arguing.

Before hailing a taxi back to the hotel, I took a long walk around the city. I was trembling with rage. It was a humiliation, an act of intimidation, an outrage to my dignity.

During my walk, I decided not to tell anyone about the incident —not Sheldon or any of the others—until we were safely over the border and there was no question of anyone seeking reprisal.

However, we were not to get over the border either easily or safely. It turned out to be a hellish nightmare, and I was to forever regret not having listened to the warnings about staying out of Zambia, as well as my own instincts concerning Hans Rohan.

The Zambian border guards, four of them, were pedantic to the point of being ridiculous. They checked our documents over and over again until we began to wonder if they were prolonging it until we offered a bribe. On the other hand they seemed so precise about the regulations that we were afraid even to hint at a payoff. They seemed slavish to the rules and asked us to fill out form after form of customs declarations. It was an enormous task because we had to list every single item in Bert's camper truck. I thought about all those guns in Hans's golf bag and wondered why it was missing today. He seemed to be carrying only an overnight case.

Despite all the custom forms, the guards insisted on searching our things. I was the first to have my luggage opened. When they went through my makeup case, they opened every single jar and bottle and even had the audacity to squeeze my toothpaste out on the counter and then tell me to clean it up. Cathy was urging us to be calm, as each country has its own regulations and we were merely visitors. I assumed she had been taught this attitude while studying to be a travel agent.

But when they refused to give Sheldon back his medication, even after having seen his doctor's certificate and epileptic identity tag, we all bombarded them with abuse.

They then became nasty and told us to get back into the camper and follow them to the local police station.

Cathy, Sheldon, and I lifted Susan back into the camper in her wheelchair, then climbed in ourselves. But Bert and Hans remained outside to argue with the guards. Hans was demanding to know why they wanted to take us to the police station and his insistence to know finally sent the guards into a huddle. I believe that until that time, they hadn't really had any specific motive in mind.

I looked from the windshield down the length of the bridge. It wasn't far to the Rhodesian side. I could see clearly the faces of the Rhodesian guards, who now and then observed us. We were the only tourists on the bridge and our camper had been stopped at the wooden barrier for the last two hours. I knew there was no way the Rhodesians could help us, as we were behind a barrier on the Zambian side. I wondered where no-man's-land began . . . just after the barrier, or would one have to reach the center of the bridge? That distance couldn't have been much more than a hundred feet.

Then we heard loud, angry voices. The guards were saying that they were going to confiscate Bert's camper: "We take you to police station for other transportation. You have got no proper papers. Your camper truck remains in Zambia."

Bert had been pacing back and forth in an effort to contain himself, but he was turning deep red with fury. I had never known Bert to be anything but soft-spoken and gentle. His anger was a terrifying thing to see and as he trudged back and forth, the bridge seemed to vibrate. His entire disability pay had been spent on his camper truck, and he prized it above everything else. Now these border guards were proposing to take it from him.

"Bill of sale! Registration! Import license!" He shook with rage as he shouted and waved the car papers in front of them. "What else do you want?"

A guard said, "Those are not stamped with recent verification."

"Therefore," another added, "we are confiscating your vehicle." Then he made a fatal mistake. He attempted to take the car keys out of Bert's hand.

Suddenly Bert exploded, his huge hands swung out, and the guard crashed backwards into the wooden customs shed.

The other three were slow to react. You could see they were in the process of thinking about drawing their pistols when Hans, who had gradually been backing up to the camper, reached underneath and whipped out a machine gun. "Do not move!" he shouted, pointing it at them, and the guards put their hands in the air.

"Let's get out of here!" Hans shouted to Bert.

The door on the driver's side flew open and Bert clambered in and started the engine. Sheldon opened the side door for Hans who, while backing up, threatened the guards to the last second. Bert gunned the motor, threw it into gear, and stepped on the gas, sending us crashing through the barricade.

It was then that two sounds overlapped: the cracking of the wooden barrier and a continuous cracking noise. I turned to see Hans at the still-open side door firing his machine gun at the Zambian guard post. And I saw Sheldon as he sprang onto Hans's back screaming, "Stop, you crazy bastard!"

At the sound of the gunfire, Bert swung his body around, turning the steering wheel sharply and veering us into a cement buttress at the side of the bridge. He braked just in time but nonetheless sent us all flying. We never knew if it was at that moment or earlier, when he had tackled Hans, that Sheldon had hit his head.

Before we reached the border, the Rhodesians had their rifles leveled at us. Hans threw his machine gun out the side door. When we were arrested, he voluntarily told them about other weapons he had secured to the underside of the camper.

Half-conscious, Sheldon was lifted out of my arms and placed in a squad car to be driven to the nearest clinic.

The rest of us were taken to police headquarters. Bert and Hans were put behind bars. After each of us had been individually interrogated, Cathy, Susan, and I were permitted to be together in the inspector's office. We were to stay there all of that night and remain there for further endless hours. We were implicated in a shooting incident and the smuggling of arms. If only there had been some conclusive way of proving that we had had no long-standing association with Hans Rohan, we might not have been detained for such a long period. By far, the worst thing for me was not knowing what was happening to Sheldon. And I was not to have news of him until after my release.

Although he had not lost complete consciousness at the moment of impact, he had remained dazed and sick to his stomach from the blow on the head. The terrifying news was that he had gone into numerous epileptic seizures. The doctors were unwilling to take responsibility for his condition. Without his medical history the clinic was afraid to prescribe anything, and all of his own medication had been confiscated by the Zambians. Once his family doctor was reached, he prescribed a temporary medication. And once Sheldon's *maman* had spoken to the authorities, they were willing to give in to her demands and put Sheldon on the first plane back to Paris.

I was informed of all this only after he had been taken from the clinic. I hadn't had a chance to speak to Sheldon directly. While I was relieved that he would be receiving proper medical care, I felt desperate that he was gone without my even having had an opportunity to speak to him or see him. It was the most brutal of partings and one that left me stunned with disbelief and grief and an intolerable sense of loss.

That despicable South African had used us. At the time we were freed unconditionally, so was he. The Rhodesians told us that he had not been aiming at the Zambians, merely shooting over their heads to keep them at bay. It was never clear to me what treatment Hans received, nor how secretly sympathetic to his cause the Rhodesians might have been. The two halves of the country were, after all, in a state of cold war.

Certainly he had used us to try and pass himself off as a harmless tourist. It occurred to me that all those so-called hunters from the lodge might well have been members of a terrorist group. They may also have used us under the guise of taking us to see native dancing in order perhaps to check out the border crossing at night. I felt in some way responsible for what happened to us because I had not heeded the very strong instinctive misgivings I had had all along about Hans Rohan. It was unbearable to me to think that my name might have been linked with that man and his organization.

I was most grateful when that did not happen. Either the inspector of police had been considerate and had not permitted the story —and in particular my name—to be given to the press, or there were other more clandestine motives of which I was unaware.

Were we delayed for that length of time because the Rhodesians were checking Hans's profile with the South African police? If so, I find it difficult to believe that they had given him a clean bill of health. Or were we in fact delayed until Hans had been identified as a secret agent for the Rhodesians? Somehow that seems more logical to me.

(The following year, I read about a terrorist who was killed while on a raid in Zambia. It was uncanny how closely the description fitted the man I have called Hans Rohan. I always have assumed it to have been him, because a large cache of arms was found stored in the walls of the place I have here referred to as the Zambezi Gorge Hunting Lodge.)

Before telephoning Paris, I considered a long while what my attitude should be, what I might say. I was at a loss to know how to alleviate either his sorrow at the parting or my own. I didn't want to upset Sheldon by becoming too emotional. We never promised that it would be forever. Sooner or later we would have had to go our separate ways . . . I, the older woman with the responsibility of teenage children and a demanding career . . . he, the romantic young boy who needed to live inside his fantasies while fleeing from one exotic location to the next, always one step ahead of the affliction which ever pursued and promised to consume him.

Even when we spoke, he was already planning a tour of China. "Have you been to China?" Sheldon was asking me for the second time.

The question had thrown me off balance. I seemed unable to reply. Then Sheldon stammered, "What do you think of the idea? I mean . . . would you?"

When he stammered, I felt miserable . . . guilty for not answering him.

Our long-distance connection had an intermittent crackle.

"Can you hear me, darling?" he asked hesitantly.

Finally, I said, "No, my darling . . . I wouldn't be able to go. I . . ." But I couldn't go on to explain. I had heard the echo of my own voice on the line. It sounded expressionless. Hollow.

He must have understood. He didn't press the subject. "I'll be leaving quite shortly . . . no doubt. I've always wanted a better look at China."

I kept asking him: "How are you, my darling? How are you feeling?" But I couldn't get him to give me a satisfactory answer. Sheldon always refused to speak seriously about his condition.

He attempted, no doubt, to ease my concern and perhaps his

own by retreating into jocularity: "I suppose I'm still mad as a hatter, my love. How are you?"

"Please tell me how you are, Sheldon."

"Well, *maman* is gushing to everyone that I'm recovering splendidly. And as is her usual remedy for everything, she is throwing an elaborate dinner party in my honor."

"But darling, what does the doctor say?"

"Oh, he's a close-mouthed fellow. He never says much of anything."

"All right then, Sheldon, what do *you* say?"

"My darling, there is not a person in Parisian society who will any longer believe a word *I* say."

I felt I shouldn't keep on nagging. I went along with his game and teased him: "Come on, my darling, tell me the truth. They don't believe a word you say because you have told too many tall stories in the past!"

"No . . ." He hesitated. "Not that many . . . but for instance, my love, *maman* has decided that I must have hit my head because of a crash in a light aircraft."

"Why would she choose to believe that?"

"Because when I told her and my father the real story . . ." Sheldon began to chuckle " . . . when I told them that we had been taken over by a terrorist and had fled across the border under machine-gun fire, they both walked out of the room in disgust!"

"I suppose truth is stranger than . . . et cetera, et cetera," I said laughing. Then I tried once again to find out if he were still ill. "Tell me, are you feeling well enough to attend a dinner party?"

"More than," he chuckled. "I'm sitting here in bed planning my entrance." He broke into hearty laughter. "Perhaps I shall arrive as Count Dracula."

"What?"

"Count Dracula."

"Dracula?"

"Yes."

"Actually the line was bad just then, but I thought you might have said Dracula."

"Yes, just think of it, my darling . . . Maman will have set the scene for her rosy-cheeked, healthy son to be greeted back from the dead . . ."

I suddenly saw the picture and began to giggle myself.

"I shall arrive in a formal black suit and opera cape. But I shan't immediately be recognized as a vampire. I'll put only tiny telltale dark circles under my eyes . . . my skin will have just a hint of sickly white . . ."

"Oh, I see." I laughed. "You're planning a delayed revelation."

"Yes, yes . . . first everyone must have time to feel pity for a mother who has delusions that her debilitated son has recovered."

"Then what . . . then what?" I asked, choking back my laughter.

"I shall then, in the weakest possible voice, offer to make a toast," he said with glee. "At which point I shall fly onto the top of the table . . . grin broadly . . . and expose bloody fangs!"

"Oh, you are naughty! It sounds wicked!" I said, still laughing.

There was a pause in the conversation.

Then I couldn't stop myself from saying: "I miss you so much. . . . if only we . . . our parting was so abrupt . . . so harsh . . . I'm finding it difficult to bear . . ."

Sheldon was silent. He was silent for such a long time that I thought perhaps we had been disconnected.

Then in a voice that was breaking, he said, "My darling, the parting could never have been easy."

If only I hadn't been so awkward! He had been brave, concealing his feelings with typical elegance and dignity. It was I who had forced his composure to crumble. Oh, how I wished I had bitten my tongue and not reduced us both to unheroic tears.

It was I who was supposed to be the mature one, the one with no more illusions and a stronger sense of self-restraint. But how do you convince yourself that a day will come when the pain begins to fade? For the moment I had no answers. I was completely inconsolable . . . Oh, God, how I missed him!

On the very same day that I had my phone conversation with Sheldon, it was also time to say good-bye to Bert, Cathy, and Susan. Again, if I had great difficulty restraining my emotions, it was because those relationships as well were coming forever to an end. It was most unlikely that we would ever see one another again. But as we hugged and kissed and openly cried, we assured one another that someday we would meet . . . by chance . . . on the veranda of the New Stanley.

I felt too distraught to fly back to Rome immediately. I telephoned Sally and Mac, and they urged me to come to Tsavo.

I knew—I must have known all along—that our romance would not outlive the rainy season. But I had expected an earthshaking storm to mark the end of our journey together. I had longed for those tears in a rainstorm and that one last embrace. And they were forever lost to me.

Yet I was unwilling to forfeit some more dramatic way of venting my sorrow. I wanted something momentous to happen to mark our parting . . . I wanted the heavens to open up as an expression of what I was feeling. And Sally and Mac, who had understood, had told me to hurry. The clouds were gathering, the big rains were definitely on their way!

Tsavo was as parched and dust-covered as the Serengeti had been the previous month. Dark rainclouds hung about but were taking a long time in giving up their precious gift. Mac took me to see the condition of the land and the level of the waterholes. It was a time of desperation for the animals, and Mac felt their suffering almost as though it were his own. The trees and shrubs had been stripped bare and there was dry stubble where not long before a rich savannah had stretched. Little was left between the animals and starvation. But mainly they were dying of exhaustion in their intensive search for food, combined with long journeys to and from the rivers: the Tiva to the north and the Galana to the south which flows from the foothills of Kilimanjaro.

It was so very, very hot. The umbrella tree gave only the thinnest canopy: barely enough to shield a cheetah, but no longer an adequate parasol for a buffalo. The fever tree was scorched and not attractive enough even for a lizard. The secretary birds, with quills over their ears like pens, no longer stayed high in the flat-topped trees, and on the ground some of the spring had gone from their step. Silverthorn was now an aged gray and it was difficult to believe that its stipules had ever been succulent.

We saw bleached bones of elephants on trails they used to arrive at their favorite watering holes. The old and infirm died first, and then others not so old but just too tired to go on. Some would succumb only hours before the lifesaving rains came to rescue all those who had been able to forbear.

The adult elephants took great care that the babies had food and water. We watched a baby knock sand into an almost depleted waterhole. Two slow-moving, nearly exhausted adults set to scooping it out.

"That's patience and love for you," Mac said. "Now watch."

One adult rubbed moist sand on the baby to cool it while the other adult put water from her trunk into its mouth.

When the adults turned to get themselves a drink, the baby stumbled and more sand slid down the banks. Wearily but without a sign of annoyance, they again scooped the sand away.

"I'm afraid, after the first mishap, I would have tied it by its little trunk to a tree or something." I laughed.

"They'll let the calf drink first no matter how thirsty they are themselves."

"Look, Mac, how much deeper they have dug that hole!"

"The elephants create them in the first place," he told me. "They roll around and dig with their trunks and make the wells. But we're hacking away at the elephants' territory. It's only a matter of time until there is no more space for them."

"I still have faith that we'll save the wildlife," I said with forced optimism. I knew that conservationists, hard as they were trying, were still fighting an uphill battle. My nightmare is that perhaps my grandchildren will never be able to see an animal in the wild, but we must keep trying to save them and never give up the fight.

"If the elephants go, I don't know how the other animals will survive," Mac said.

"What do you mean?"

"If the elephants go, the others have no means of digging wells and trapping rainwater," Mac said. "Three years ago rain fell about a hundred kilometers from here, but not at the lodge, and the elephants disappeared overnight. They can smell the rain, you know, and can make the journey. Without them to keep the holes dug out, we had carcasses everywhere. Dead lions beside dead wildebeests."

There was an enormous beige cloud covering half the horizon now but no humidity in the air, and when a breeze came up the dust rose in great sheets similar to a sandstorm. But we heard rumblings in the north and knew it was only a question of time before relief came.

Few guests were at the lodge and they would all be leaving tomorrow or the day after, or the minute after the rains came. The rains would last approximately three weeks and the MacKennas always went home to visit Sally's family in Scotland at that time. As Sally put it, they would "Batten down the hatches in the wilderness and go back to the refinements of civilization."

Shortly after we had finished lunch, a powerful duststorm blew and we were forced to leave the terrace and have our coffee in the shelter of the MacKennas' apartment. As I looked up, I saw heavy rainclouds gathering and I felt the incredible drama inherent in the approach to the rainy season.

On the way to my room after coffee, I noticed that the sky had turned almost black, and yet the earth was glowing in a clearer-than-clear brightness. There was a change in the air which I could feel and almost taste. The mournful cry of the rainbird had become a continuous wail, and I longed so much to share it all with Sheldon.

At teatime, heavy drops began a slow bombardment. They struck the parched earth and bounced like resilient pearls, I thought. Seconds later the duststorm was obliterated by sharp raindrops that pierced the air, falling straight as knives. Months of progressive dryness were suddenly at an end. The heavens opened up and a dense sheet of water descended.

The heavens opened up . . . now I witnessed the meaning of that phrase. I had to tell Sheldon. I sat down to write him a letter. I would tell him everything I was feeling . . . everything? No, I mustn't . . . not everything . . . just how the heavens opened up.

Perhaps half an hour passed in which the deluge continued. Then I heard the sound of the storm change once more to heavy drops and I glanced up. When I looked back down at my writing table there was a winged insect, half an inch long, on my letter. I heard faint noises behind my chair and, looking around, saw three or four of the same insects struggling to move over the wooden floor, trailing their wings behind them as if they were cripples. I returned to my letter and now there were five or six more on my writing table. They were multiplying by the fraction of a second! Their flailing sounds were becoming almost a flapping. My doors and windows were tightly secured and I couldn't see a single crack anywhere from which they might be entering. No, they seemed to be materializing out of thin air!

Soon almost every square inch of my room was filled with them. Suddenly, as if by a miracle, they rose in flight. They began swarming all around me and then, to my horror, all over me. I tried to escape to the outside, but when I opened the door, I ran into a wall of them, a thick mass of swirling, droning insects.

I slammed the door, leaned against it and breathed deeply. Then I ran to the bed, tore the mosquito netting from the canopy and draped it over myself. In order to keep my reason, I decided to try and concentrate on nothing but my letter to Sheldon.

Shortly, another downpour began. The insects fell crippled to the floor, then disappeared. Vanished!

I was to learn that the Africans call them flying ants, and apparently they are hatched, learn to fly, breed and die, all within the brief span of a storm's interval.

I didn't want to remain alone any longer. I prepared to make a dash to the MacKennas' apartment the instant the next interval in the storm approached.

When I stepped outside, I encountered what might have been meant in the Bible by a plague. In every direction as far as the eye could see there was an oozing carpet of mud and struggling frogs: frogs of every size, color, and shape. So prolific were they that there was not enough space for all of them and they were climbing on top of one another as they tried to extricate themselves from the sucking, gurgling marsh.

"I swear those frogs were not there when I first opened the door," I told Sally, Mac, and their five guests. "They materialized sometime during the second downpour."

Mac laughed. "Most of the frogs burrow underground until the dry spell is over. Then just as soon as the earth is softened by the rains, they struggle up to the surface."

"This first night of the rains seems to belong to them," Sally said. "Just wait until you hear the frog chorus when they arrive at the watering holes."

"Who is game for a great show?" Mac asked. "We could throw on some raingear and see the opera going on in nature!"

"It is very exciting to see what happens on the first evening of the rains," Sally added. "And I'm afraid dinner is hardly worth sitting down to, as we can only offer you some beer and sandwiches."

Three of the guests opted to stay behind with their beer and sandwiches, preferring to play cards. That meant that Sally, Mac, and I, along with the one remaining couple, were all able to go in Mac's Land Rover.

Although the sun was hidden, the sky was still light at six o'clock. Mac had the top up on the Land Rover but the windows were open. All of a sudden it poured again and we got drenched. I didn't mind; in fact, I loved it. Everything was exciting and dramatic, just what I felt I needed.

Mac kept to high ground wherever possible, being cautious about the possibility of flash-flooding. Indeed, there must have been exceptionally heavy rain upstream because the outlets from the Galana were raging torrents. Even the crocodiles had left the water in order not to be swept away.

All elephant trails lead to watering holes, and now the trails themselves had become streams rushing to fill the wells. The animals would no longer have to make those exhausting treks to the river. As early as tomorrow or the next day one would see fresh vegetation sprouting. The expectancy in the air was the imminence of life returning to the plains.

The next morning as I flew over Tsavo on my way back to Nairobi I could detect distinct green in the landscape. The herds seemed revived and full of spirit . . . I'm not sure why, but I began crying.

Then a fresh downpour obstructed my view, and I calculated at what hour I would be on the veranda of the New Stanley to endure my next good-bye, this one to Africa. "Oh, Sheldon," I said quietly to myself, "I think perhaps I am already missing Africa . . . And oh, Sheldon, I miss you."

And I would miss him for a long, long time to come. On nights when I would wake up crying for him there would be no one to tell, except perhaps my diary. Then, so often his spirit, defying captivity, would not allow itself to be committed to my page. For if at times Sheldon had appeared tame, his spirit was beyond containment or repression.

He was whimsical, capricious, original . . . totally spontaneous and wildly eccentric . . . but he was also sweet and precious and loving, and in his own uniquely "loony" way, he was most definitely magical.

Even after all the years that would pass, when there would inevitably be other men, other loves, I would treasure the memories of those few months we had had together. And Sheldon would always remain one of those people whom I have loved too well ever to forget.